The Phoenix
and the albatross

CHAPTER I

Since I was a child, I have always had two dreams in life: one to be a great writer and the other to be able to visit the Galapagos and watch the sunset on its beaches with a loved one. However, it is not so easy to fulfill dreams. Life is not like fairy tales. There are no fairy godmothers that appear to fix nightmares with the wave of a wand and I have made too many mistakes considering that I am only twenty-one years old and I have just finished my studies as a designer.

I wish I had studied literature or journalism. Then I could be closer to one of my two dreams, but when you live in a poor neighborhood in Istanbul and your parents have trouble paying the bills at the end of the month with their butcher shop, you have to focus on reality. At least it could be worse. My future could be surrounded by sausage and minced meat with parents who seem to be competing to drive me crazy.

But now I have an opportunity to save up and move to a Greek island. You have to be modest and sometimes it's better to switch to more achievable goals.

Last week my friend Ayhan showed me an ad in the newspaper: they were looking for designers to work in a film studio with a bombastic name. It didn't ring a bell. The company must have been set up by a rich old man who probably spends his nights looking for excuses to approach models. The salary they offer is good, so that's why today I'm in an office with other girls who are probably better prepared for this job than me.

I keep biting my nails. It's a defect I picked up thanks to my mother's nagging. It was either that or set the house on fire. But, well, I look decent. I put on my best dress and went to Melahat's hair salon, who went crazy when I told her I was going to my first job interview and went on and on about how she used to do my hair when I was a kid while she was fixing my ends.

I sigh. They just called the girl who sat next to me. I look at my portfolio of internship designs and my small, almost insignificant resume. I'm tempted to walk out and tell my parents I failed the test. Better that than embarrass myself at the interview.

-Sanem Aydin! -A long-legged secretary who might as well work as an actress calls out to me.

I swallow. For a second, I'm tempted to pretend I don't know any Sanem Aydin, but I stand up on clumsy feet that look like baby elephants. The actress secretary leads me into a room decorated with posters of movie stars and show commercials. With a shudder I sit down. Across from me are two men who also look like something out of a Hollywood movie.

One of them looks at other resumes and passes them by reluctantly. What will he think of mine? The other one watches me carefully, giving me a smile that I'm sure he gives to all the knuckleheads just out of college. They're both damned attractive. The one who asks my name and encourages me to sit down has the image of the perfect gentleman. He's the kind of guy who gets invited to the most pedigreed parties and who all mothers fantasize about marrying their daughters off to. His companion, on the other hand, seems more suitable for an evening in a night bar, the typical conqueror who seduces young girls with beautiful words, typical of a poet, and who says goodbye the next morning without leaving a single phone number.

-It's a pleasure to meet you, Miss Aydin-, says the gentleman who shakes my hand while the other absentmindedly fixes his lustrous hair.

-My name is Emre Divit and I am the personnel manager and this is my brother, Can Divit, the director of the project for which we are interviewing you. According to your resume, you're a recent graduate. Is this the first interview you've applied for?

Oh no. That question can only mean they're looking for someone with experience. A famous designer that studios are fighting over and graduated with full honors. At what point did it occur to me that this was a good idea?

-Yes, Mr. Divit... However, I have brought copies of my portfolio with some of my designs from college.

I leave them on the table without opening the folder. Maybe I don't have to be embarrassed anymore and this will move on to the next candidate, but the gallant man picks up my designs and examines them. He smiles. For a second I forget the embarrassment and the rage eats me up inside. I didn't need to be shown that I'm useless in such a graphic way.

-When did you make these designs, Miss Aydin?

-They are all final projects-, I answer without hesitation. If I'm only here for a short time, I must maintain my dignity.

-Interesting. Do you like literature?

What did you think I was? A knucklehead who was just a pretty face?

-Yes, I specialized in cover design, layout and advertising campaigns in that field, although I'm adaptable to any field.

-Oh, I see you did a design for a BBC television adaptation.

-Yes, *Emma*, by Jane Austen. She's one of my favorite authors.

-And you like poetry?

I sighed. Yes.

-Do you know Baudelaire?

I look at his brother. He's as out of it as I am. Can Divit must be the black sheep of the family.

-Of course. I've read The Flowers of Evil several times.

The jackal's grin widens and he leaves my designs on the table. His brother takes the opportunity to take a look at them.

-For distraction, sometimes sailors hunt albatrosses, great birds of the sea....

-Who follow, indolent traveling companions, the ship furrowing the bitter abysses-, I conclude. I have seldom felt so much pleasure in taking advantage of my photographic memory as I do at this moment. -I can recite any poem if you wish to test me, Mr. Divit.

Can bursts out laughing. His brother nods as he looks at the designs. I like his approval, but now I'm afraid of being hired. I don't want to imagine having to put up with the literature-loving seducer as my boss.

-You have a prodigious mind, Miss Aydin. I've rarely seen such sensitivity in designs and I've traveled the world as a professional photographer. Only a photograph can aspire to freeze the unrepeatable beauty of a poem.

I recognize that this phrase has caused me a spark of admiration. Just a tiny one.

-I don't think there's no need for any more interviews, Emre. Miss Aydin has the job.

-But Can. We've arranged six more interviews-, his brother protested.

-I'll take care of apologizing to the other candidates personally. I don't think it's necessary to waste their time.

I'm about to have a fit. I have to control myself not to hyperventilate, although I think poor Emre is more shocked than I am. Can leaves the office and I hear his deep voice behind the door I don't understand his words until he comes back to say:

-Tonight we are having a company party with the employees. It would be my pleasure if you could attend, Miss Aydin.

As I recover from the shock, Emre Divit smiles at me.

-Excuse my brother, Miss Aydin. He is a free spirit, so to speak. He is uncontrollable, but the truth is that your designs show great creativity. This must be one of his more lucid decisions-, he notes warmly as he shakes my hand again, welcoming me into the company.

Back at home, I feel like I'm on cloud nine. On the one hand, I still can't believe I finally have a job. I'll be able to help at home with the bills and even uptight Leyla will admit that I'm a responsible and mature person, that I don't have a head full of birds and I don't think only about books, although Literature has a unique magic as Can Divit said. I snort. The best thing to do was to forget about that man. Surely I would never see him again and we would deal with all professional matters by e-mail.

At home, my parents greet me with a warm hug and pepper me with questions about the interview. I avoid talking about Can and mention to-night's party in passing. On the way out, the secretary tells me where the event will take place: in one of the most prestigious hotels in Istanbul. What a change my life has taken with a simple interview. Is this the adult life everyone is talking about?

Mom calls Leyla to tell her the happy news and, oh dear, I find out that she's coming too. Apparently, her firm has also been hired by the Divit brothers' studio, so, by a twist of fate, we're going to be co-workers. I'd almost rather have Can Divit as an office mate.

As I get dressed up and change from my first-job-seeking graduate dress to a party dress, I can't help but think of Baudelaire's poem, The Albatross. The albatross is an elegant bird, an animal that spends almost all the time of its life flying, indestructible, and only returns to its home, the Galapagos Islands to mate, to know love.

I suffocate. A high-class party is not a suitable place for me. I feel more comfortable among books, designing, watching the birds flying into the Sea of Marmara and getting lost in the Istanbul sunset.

In front of the standing mirror in my room, there is a stranger dressed up for a gala party. She smiles shyly at me, though she wonders if she is ready for the real thing.

CHAPTER II

Leyla and I do not speak to each other. We take a cab to the Dersaadet hotel. Earlier, she asked me a hundred thousand times not to make a fool of her in front of the Divit brothers. She gave me a very boring talk about how influential this family is and how important it is for her company that this film studio project goes ahead.

She has also prepared for the party and is the spitting image of a fairytale princess, although her attitude is more like that of a harpy. Luckily, the cab ride doesn't take long and we soon find ourselves in the midst of beautiful people laughing anodyne laughs as they clink champagne glasses.

Leyla comfortably immerses herself in this atmosphere and I have to manage to find my own little spot. Since I'm on edge, I go in search of some Turkish tea, but find nothing, except for a funny character named Ceycey who is the studio's caterer.

-Hey, Sanem, what are you going to do in the company?

-I'll be the advertising design manager-, I answer sheepishly.

-Ah, so you're the one who has captivated Can. You must be spectacularly talented.

It's obvious that Ceycey has a few too many drinks. We start talking about the people passing in front of us, imagining their positions and personalities, until Leyla crosses our path.

-She looks like the spoiled child of the family. I'm sure she works as a secretary for an important boss and does everything right in her job.

-You're absolutely right-, I reply with a laugh. -Although you forgot to add that she's my sister.

Ceycey rolls his eyes like a frightened lamb. I love it. It's nice to be able to end the day talking to a human being who can feel emotions.

-Don't worry. We're nothing alike. I'm sure she's adopted, but my parents won't confirm it.

Leyla turns to me with a frown, and now I look like I've never broken a dish in my life. After five minutes, Ceycey mumbles something about having to go to the restroom and I say goodbye with an affectionate pat on the back. Distracted, I stroll among the party guests and inadvertently bump into some eighty-year-old bigwig who looks at me like I'm a circus critter. Relieved, I realize that there is no sign of Can. The only member of the Divit family who deigns to show his company to the others is good old Emre, who meets an old man whom he looks at with admiration and to whom he keeps introducing people. With the experience gained with Ceycey, I intuit that it is his father, the famous patriarch Divit, although this man, unlike his brothers, inspires me a little pity. He looks tired, although he tries to hide it by smiling warmly at his guests. However, when a stunning woman in a white dress that makes her look like a swan appears before him, his expression changes.

People murmur as they shout.

-Aylin. Please go away-, Emre pleads.

-Don't worry. I just wanted to say goodbye to what I thought was my family," the woman replies with spite and a sly smile, basking in the hatred that disfigures Mr. Divit's expression.

She leaves like a diva. And Emre pretends she doesn't exist. His expression is desolate and furious, though not like his father's. My instinct whispers to me that there is a broken heart behind that scowl.

Out of discretion, I walk away. The party atmosphere disappears and, as I can't think of what to talk about with the cream of Istanbul's crop, I go in search of Leyla or Ceycey. Either one will do.

I open doors in search of a bathroom because I imagine poor Ceycey's bladder will have been put to the test with so much alcohol, although I don't know how I end up in a darkened room. The air is calm in there. It looks like a prince's bedchamber because I smell flowers and a scent I can't quite identify. I step through the shadows that embrace me, and suddenly I find myself surrounded by two flesh-and-blood, muscular, romance-hero arms, and a sweet kiss lands on my lips.

My breathing stops, though it then matches the gentle beating of my heart. I want to reciprocate the kiss because that affection makes me feel at home at last, but sanity forces me to pull away from my wonderful stranger.

-Who are you? -he asks.

Of course. That kiss was not for me, even though that seductive voice brings back sweet memories. I run out of that forbidden passage, returning to the hotel lobby where I was supposed to be enjoying a company party.

By the canapes table, Leyla is scanning the surroundings like a bird of prey. She was looking for me, too. Feigning naturalness, I head towards her, although I end up bumping into two other people, earning a disdainful gesture from my dear sister.

-Have you been drinking? -she asks me with her nasty retort.

Normally I retort, proving to her that I'm not the one with no brains in the family, but now I can only express in babbles.

-Let's go home. It's late and the Divits are nervous.

I nod and let myself be led like a sweet little lamb to the cab. Leyla is in her own world, though she gives me disapproving glances from time to time. I turn on my cell phone. Maybe I'll distract myself by playing a game or chatting with someone. When I turn it on, lots of messages light up my screen. It's my friend Ayhan. My mother must have told the whole neighborhood that I've been hired and burned my cell phone with missed calls. I startle when my phone vibrates, thinking it's going to explode, but it's only Ayhan, calling me again.

-Hello? -I answer.

-What's wrong, Sanem? -my friend asks, alarmed.

-What are you saying?

-Something happened to you, Sanem, and it's not because of the new job. Where are you now?

Oh, my God. I just remembered who's with me. Leyla keeps eavesdropping on my conversation.

-Coming home in a cab. With Leyla. We were at a company party.

-At a party? With Leyla? You have to tell me everything.

Ayhan was talking like a machine gun. In her head she must have been spinning a story that could be dangerously close to reality.

-No, nothing happened...-, she whispered.

-Oh! You've met a boy. Yes, that must be it. Is that it?

-No...

-You made out with someone!!!

-What are you talking about? -I stammer, remembering that familiar voice and that kiss that you could only receive when you are loved.

-Okay. With Leyla you can't tell me anything. We'll talk later. Now come to your senses-, she lets go of me and hangs up the phone.

I turn to Leyla as if I'm distracted. My sister raises an eyebrow, as she always does when she judges me.

-That was Ayhan. She was calling to ask me about work.

-And that's why you were whispering? Well, I'd rather not hear your stories. I hope you didn't make a mess.

Always the same. Was I that bad at lying? And Mom says my imagination is out of this world. Maybe I'm in the wrong dream to be a writer. I should focus on something I'm good at, like... I don't know. I'll figure something out. Or maybe I shouldn't give up writing. Wasn't love one of the main sources of inspiration for art? But I wasn't in love. A stranger with a seductive voice had embraced me mistaking me for someone. That tender and sincere kiss was for someone else, a woman like the beauties I had passed at the party.

I take a deep breath. I breathe in and out, ignoring Leyla. And I remember a quote about love and I think about that feeling that is born in my chest. Reason tells me it's a stupid and unfounded emotion, but as Orhan Pamuk said, maybe true love is the one you feel for someone you don't see. Loving without seeing awakens other senses. The physical aspect loses importance. You only remember smells, sounds, tastes; I remember everything. I remember that voice that asked me who I was, that was not angry with me, but that was interested in me, to know me in depth and in my head I think that I have fallen in love with you without seeing you, sweet stranger. I know I will dream of you every day, of your hands and your face. I don't care. I only ask you to come find me, look at me, stay with me.

God, had I been drinking while chatting with Ceycey? I don't remember. All that's present in my head is a kiss that wasn't meant for me, but that fate was determined to give me. I shouldn't have been hired at a thriving film studio. My resume was ridiculous. That party was the perfect setting for girls like Leyla. However, I was there. I pushed through the darkness, making my way to a man who knew what the word love meant.

-Sanem, wake up. Sanem! -my sister shrieks, shaking me.

The cab is stopped in front of my parents' house. The living room lights are on. They're probably waiting to ask us how everything went. Oh, no. My mother hunts down my lies as if she had been trained as a child to do so.

Leyla drags me home. Dad reads the paper and Mom cleans the kitchen, but when we arrive they approach us to bombard us with questions about the party.

-What's wrong, Sanem? -says my mother. She grabs my face and analyzes it. I guess she thinks I had a few too many drinks at the party, too.

-Nothing. I'm just tired. There were a lot of people and it's hard for me to socialize with strangers.

With that excuse, they leave me alone and I lock myself in my room. A second later, my phone lights up with Ayhan's call.

-Hello...- I answer, letting go of the air that was clinging to my chest.

-Tell me everything, Sanem-, my friend demands.

How could I explain that movie kiss? Words were insufficient to convey the moment the stranger and I shared.

-Nothing. I've been hired as a designer at a new film studio. One of the directors liked my design, hired me and invited me to a company party. I met a really nice guy, his name is Ceycey, and I got lost because the bosses started yelling at a woman. I went looking for him, I went into a dark room and there was... there was... there was a man who hugged me. Oh, Ayhan, I've never been hugged like that before and that kiss....

I took refuge in Ayhan's verbiage as I remembered the kiss from the stranger I would surely never see again.

-Who was he? He must have been an employee of your company.

-I don't know. He was strong, muscular. With a beard. I felt protected. He was my albatross.

-Albatross?

I don't know why I associated the kiss with the poem Can Divit mentioned to me, but the words flowed on their own, as they do in the best novels.

-It's a powerful bird, one that can't get enough. I felt so protected, Ayhan. Did you know that the albatross flies for most of its life? It only returns home to go back to its beloved and the rest of the time it is at sea.

I don't know if one day I will be able to go to the Galapagos, although for a few seconds that night I found my little personal paradise, a little corner where I knew love, a unique feeling, not a whim like the one Misifú, the neighbor's son, has with me, who since he knows how to say two words together tries to conquer me with an I love you. Oh, my God. I wish it were like that. Misifú only mumbles embarrassing phrases from cheap novels with which he thinks he can seduce me. Poor thing. Actually, I feel sorry for him. He thinks I'm a special girl because he hasn't dared to look beyond me, to other girls who appreciate the way he is, who long to hear his words of love.

I go to bed. Tomorrow is my first day at work. Maybe I'll meet my mystery gentleman again and he'll recognize me. He will say that he didn't really expect anyone but me. That he loves me and doesn't want to be separated from me.

My goodness. I'm sure Ceycey and I drank a bottle between the two of us. That alone would explain my stupefaction over a kiss. A little kiss. A fleeting one.

I'd never been kissed like that before. One that screamed I love you.

CHAPTER III

The sound of the alarm clock gets me out of bed as if the days of college have returned. With a yawn, I lean out the window and in the streets shopkeepers are going about their business to start their day. Mine will begin in an hour and a half. The studio is close to home, so I have time to get ready and dress in a more comfortable outfit than last night.

At breakfast, toast tastes like warm lips and my cheeks yearn for the pleasant feel of my albatross's beard. I pour myself a nice glass of tea to calm my nerves. It's for my first day on the job, nothing else. The doorbell, though, jolts me out of my reverie. I peek out to see who it is. My father must be getting ready to open the butcher shop and there's no sign of my mother. It is most likely Leyla because she has forgotten her keys.

I greet the visitor and am stunned to see that it is one of my father's suppliers.

-Good morning, Sanem. May I speak to your father?

I gesture for him to lower his voice. My mother's ear rivals the ear of a bat.

-My father has gone to work-, I whisper, hastily imagining an excuse for him not to go to the butcher shop. I bet my hand he's coming to collect debts from the business. I wish I had been hired earlier to help pay the bills. -We'll settle the debt right away. Please leave everything to me. I've just been hired at a film studio and soon...

-Sanem, you've been giving me the runaround for weeks. Your family owes me forty thousand lire and if I don't get the money soon, I'm going to denounce you. In fact, I don't know why I'm talking to you. I'm going to the butcher's.

-No! Please! -I beg you. I'm about to get down on my knees in front of him. -If you give me a bit of time, I assure you I will collect the money and talk to my father, but please don't harass him. He has a heart condition and the stress could take its toll. The business is picking up and we will have the payments up to date. I'm begging you. Trust me.

The supplier tries to get rid of me. However, I cross his path as many times as it takes to get him to notice me.

-All right, Sanem. I'll give you a week. If you don't pay me again, I'll sue you.

He leaves and I go back to my house. My mother sings a bolero from a famous TV series. Luckily she hasn't heard anything, so I shout goodbye to her so she can hear me and head to work while I think about my salary. It's a decent salary and after a year I could save the forty thousand lire we owe. The problem is that the supplier has only given me a week. Where am I going to get such a huge amount? I can't ask the bank for a loan. My parents would find out. If I ask Leyla for help, she would take care of everything and earn a lot of money, but she would lose part of her savings and she has worked very hard to become independent.

Still overwhelmed, I walk into the office. Ceycey greets me from his desk. He tells me that besides being in charge of film catering, he also controls the office equipment department.

-Can you handle it all by yourself? -I ask him.

-What can I do? We're like pixies. The studio is new, so we're moonlighting. It'll be the same for you. Watch out for Deren, the personnel manager. I think she dreams of getting a whip for Christmas.

I laugh. I wish my desk was next to his. I take my leave to introduce myself to Deren so she can point me to my desk and assign me my first tasks. I'm like a flan. My new boss wastes no time in yelling at two coworkers with fuss. She doesn't seem like a bad person, although I'm sure I can drive her crazy like I do my mom. So I remember to be attentive and diligent to save myself the problems I have at home.

-The new designer? -Deren asks me without paying attention to me. Her reports are more interesting for her.

-Yes, I'm Sanem....

-Yes, yes, the new one-, she replies. -We don't have any assignments for you for now, as we haven't hired actors and we haven't finished the production contracts. You will be my new assistant and you will be in charge of making sure that the office cafeteria is ready for the employees. If someone asks you for a coffee, you'll make it for them and you'll make sure the caterer doesn't make mistakes in the menus. Lately they don't bring us what we order.

Are you kidding me? There was nothing like that in my contract, nor did the Divit brothers tell me I was going to be the new studio maid. However, she doesn't give me time to reply and plants a mountain of folders in my hands. It almost knocks me to the floor.

-Hand these over to Mr. Divit.

-Which one? -I ask, barely keeping my balance.

-To Mr. Emre-, she replies as if I were an idiot. What a first day I have ahead of me.

I leave, even though I haven't asked her where Emre's office is. I wander around looking for Mr. Divit, feigning confidence, even though I must look like a dizzy duck. Ceycey crosses my path.

-Where are you going? -he mumbles.

-To Mr. Emre's office-, I answer in the same way.

-Down the hall. The door on the left.

Ceycey is an angel from heaven, a tiny little brown one, but the most adorable of them all. I head for Emre's office and hear Deren's voice, shouting at me not to waste any more time.

-I'm coming, ma'am! -I reply, turning around in front of Emre's office and rushing in.

I'm stunned to see Can smiling at me.

-Were you looking for me, Sanem?

I stammer.

-I'm sorry, Mr. Divit. Do you know where your brother is?

-In the office next door-, he answers with a smirk.

I snort. I hastily excuse myself, though, and on my way out, I realize I've entered the door on the right. I walk through the right door and behind it Emre Divit is arguing with someone on the phone. He looks at me quizzically and I show him the folders as if they were a white flag. Understanding, he points to his desk and I extricate myself from my burden. I escape from there on tiptoe.

-Newbie!!! -Deren calls me back. God, Sanem is not a very complicated name. It only has two syllables. -Come here!!!!

I obey like a faithful puppy and my new task as an intern is to hand out a series of brochures to all employees. It's a dossier with the company's first project. I suppose there will be one for me too, unless the new one doesn't need it to carry the coffees. Oh, I could really use a cup of tea, although I took a look at the cafeteria menu and there are a thousand different types of coffees and vegan snacks, but not a single Turkish one. I don't even order a Chinese tea!

At noon I sit at my desk, exhausted. I've never run a marathon, though I suppose it ends with the same exhaustion. I fan myself with a dossier. In the end, there was one for the new girl.

-Would you like a fresh cup of coffee, Sanem? -Ceycey asks me. Next to him is one of my new colleagues who is certainly not the errand girl.

-A tea... I just want a tea. If I hear the word coffee again, I'll smash the pot-, I assure them.

-Oh, Sanem. You're so funny- Ceycey says as if he's joking. -Meet Güliz.

-Coffee with milk. Three teaspoons of sugar. Lukewarm-, I chuckle.

Güliz lets out the same nervous chuckle as Ceycey.

-Denen has burned you on the first day. Poor thing-, the girl says without mockery. Well, this one might be nice. -Don't worry. Can is very excited about the first project and I'm sure you'll be getting orders for yours soon.

-Güliz knows everything that goes on in the office-, Ceycey explains to my astonished face.

I get a call. I startle as if my phone were a bomb.

-Sanem-, Mr. Emre calls me, but I answer the call.

-Hello?

Ceycey and Güliz flee discreetly, but Mr. Emre stays at a safe distance.

-Sanem? I have to talk to you.

Damn it. Dad's supplier. You'd think I'd signed a pact with the devil.

-I can't do it right now. I'm at work and I told him I'd give you the money this week. Yes, the forty thousand lire. I know. Trust me.

Mr. Emre listens to me worried, although he tries to pretend indifference. I get hot with embarrassment. My God, I can't wait to hang up.

-Yes, I heard you. I'll pay you by check-, I say, as long as I don't make a scene in front of my boss and say goodbye. Just in case, I turn off my cell phone.

-Excuse me, Mr. Divit.

As Emre is a gentleman, he smiles at me as if he hadn't heard anything humiliating.

23

-Don't worry, Sanem. Will you come with me to my office? I need to talk to you for a moment.

I nod. With dread. I'm sure I've screwed up some of the stupid tasks Deren gave me. However, my boss is an individual who conveys confidence and security with his smile. However, he is not like his brother. He knows how to keep up appearances. He offers me a seat at his desk to say goodbye with total elegance.

-I'm sorry you can't show your talent right now, Sanem. The studio is restructuring our family business and we are currently understaffed. However, there is one task I would like to entrust to you. An important task.

-Oh, no, sir-, I interrupt him before he makes a big mistake. -My specialty is design and I have no experience in other areas. It would be a disaster. Surely there are more qualified people in the office.

-You mustn't be so modest, Sanem. I know your sister. We have worked with her company and I have found her to be a very efficient person. For a while she was my assistant in image matters. Hasn't she told you?

What about Leyla. Always so brilliant, with a talent suited to make me look more useless than I am.

-No, sir. She's very professional and doesn't usually talk to me about her work.

-A great quality. As you said, Sanem, a very professional quality and I'm sure you share that characteristic with your sister. Also, Can believes in your potential and has asked me to entrust you with this important task.

I can't think of how to reply to Emre's kind words, so I nod.

-We need you to keep an eye on some very important documentation for our company. We have had cases of espionage in the past and we don't want details of this new project to leak out.

-Sir, this is a very important assignment. I am just a simple designer with no experience... I can't...

-Sanem-, my boss whispers to me gently. -It's true that we didn't hire you for this. That's why...-, He takes a pen out of his Italian branded jacket and reaches for the checkbook in front of his computer... -I think with this assignment you deserve a separate salary. Did you need forty thousand lire? Here it is.

I look at the cashier's check. Mr. Emre doesn't lie. I open my eyes and strain my eyes. It's not an illusion. He has written me a check for forty thousand lire with which my family's debts will be settled.

-I can't accept it. It's a year's salary....

-Sanem, I expect you to stay with this company for more than a year. That's why I've entrusted you with this job. Please, my brother and I think you're the right person.

I don't want to. I don't think I'm the right girl for such a delicate job. Still, my hand takes the check my boss offers me.

I don't feel able to give it back to him because, in spite of everything, my parents need me the most.

As I leave Emre's office, a thousand eyes are watching me, though my colleagues are adept at disguising themselves. Ceycey looks worried and asks me what Mr. Emre wanted from me.

-He just wanted to take an interest in my first day.

-He's nothing like Deren. Emre is a very caring and generous person.

I couldn't agree more with Ceycey. However, Mr. Divit's generosity makes me uncomfortable. There is no reasoning to think that I am the ideal employee to guard company secrets, except that Emre, unlike Can, is a man who always thinks the best of everyone, unlike his brother, who enjoys looking down on people. And, speaking of the king of Rome, Can is talking to Deren. To him, she doesn't yell at him or treat him like

25

he's an idiot, and to her, he doesn't smile smugly, but kindly.

He is presumptuous, though because I am an idiot as I stare at his beard I remember my mysterious albatross and the kiss that makes me for a moment forget my fears and my heart soften.

CHAPTER IV

I dare not return home and stroll along the harbor. Earlier I spoke to my father's supplier and handed him the check for forty thousand lire after making sure the debt was cleared. If someone had told me last week that I was going to secure the future of the family butcher shop thanks to my work, I would have laughed in his face, but now I look out over the waters of the Bosphorus thinking of the changes my life has taken and of a kiss, a single kiss that makes everything else seem a trifle.

I try to remember. My albatross is a colleague in my company. Someone who was in a darkened room next to the foyer at the whim of fate and apart from his smell and the taste of his lips, the only feature by which I can identify him is his beard. That would help me rule out candidates. Does it matter now though, with the new job Mr. Emre has given me?

I start my second day tomorrow and I feel like I've been in the studio for months. I sigh. Better to go home, listen to one of my parents' lover's arguments and put up with Leyla's questions about my first day. Perhaps, Ayhan also calls me to get more information out of me about my albatross, though I've barely had time to think about him today.

The moon watches me, beautiful, oblivious to my daydreams about a man whose name I don't know. It's not like I'm a teenager. Actually, I've always been a girl unlucky in love, the only one who has ever loved me is Misifú, my childhood friend, and I can't even call him by name, and I think of him as if he were stupid. Poor Muzaffer.

I go back to my family, to my routine, and as I lie in bed I no longer think about debts or espionage issues, only about love.

The next day, I say goodbye to mom and accompany dad to the butcher shop to make sure the supplier is not still bothering him. At the office, Deren again has me handing out folders that I am not allowed to look at and Mr. Emre has called me to tell me that I will start as Can's assistant after a meeting after lunch.

During a break, Ceycey approaches me worriedly with Güliz.

-What's wrong, Sanem?

I turn around like a cat being approached with a jug of water.

-What's wrong with me? I've gone back to work as an errand girl for a harpy who can't memorize a name as simple as Sanem. Then, if I'm lucky, I'll get to be the assistant of a man in love with himself who amuses himself by smiling at me as if I were a fool, even though according to him I have the talent for a job for which I haven't been asked yet.

Ceycey and Güliz make funny faces. I don't care. I'm blurting out like a machine gun what I would have liked to shout at Deren and Can.

-And on top of that, they're all such gentlemen here. I'd have a tea to relax but oh, surprise, people here only drink export coffee and they look like they're going to die if they eat anything with more calories than lettuce leaves.

-Sanem...-, mutters Ceycey.

-No, Ceycey, I'm letting off steam because we're being run by a bunch of smug tyrants.

-Let it all out, Sanem. Yes, sir. I want to hear everything you think-, Can Divit lets go behind me.

I almost choke just breathing. Can watches me with one of his all-control grins, amused by the situation. He looks me in the eye, daring me to keep ranting at him, but I need the job, especially after the mess I've gotten myself into with Mr. Emre.

-I... just...

-No need to say more, Sanem. I'll wait for you at the staff meeting. Don't be unpunctual-, he says goodbye, though he's only talking to me.

When he leaves, there is silence. Neither Ceycey nor Güliz dares to encourage me with meaningless words.

-He's going to fire me-, I affirm when I remember how they speak to each other.

Ceycey shrugs. For the first time he doesn't know what to say. Until the meeting, I concentrate on being the most obedient puppy for Deren. I write reports. I carry folders. For this job, all you need to do is keep your mouth shut and know how to carry things like a burrito. And that's not even what I've been good at.

When it's time for the meeting, the staff gathers around Mr. Can and watches him nervously. The director exudes charisma and knows how to keep his audience quiet. He is not dressed in a suit and tie like Mr. Emre, but wears an outfit fit for an evening in a trendy bar in Istanbul's wealthy neighborhoods.

-Good morning, everyone. I hope I'm not taking up too much of your time-, he says with false humility. -Ugh, my mouth is dry. Sila, can you bring me a glass of tea, please?

-There is no tea, Mr. Can-, Deren explains nervously.

-Why is that?

-Because we have the best coffees on the cafeteria menu.

-But there is nothing better than a good Turkish tea-, he replies.

-That's what I think too-, I jump up from my seat.

Can smiles. He's a braggart who doesn't know how to keep his manners in a company, and so is my boss. Maybe with a bit of luck he'll forget what I said earlier with Ceycey and Güliz. However, my colleagues are watching me. I'm like the crazy woman who just escaped from the mental hospital.

-Sanem, sit down now-, my friend encourages me in whispers.

-Deren, bring two teas, please-, Can orders as I slowly sit down. Calmly, so as not to draw more attention to myself.

Although ten minutes later I have to be careful that the saucer holding my cup of tea doesn't make too much noise as it shakes in my lap. Instead, Can enjoys his brew and exudes comfort.

-I'm sorry for the delay. Anyway, the matter that has prompted me to call this meeting is brief. As you may know, this studio was founded out of our old advertising agency. Many of you have come from there and I would like to say that I have full confidence in all of you, but we have a spy in the company who leaks our projects to competing companies and we fear that this could be repeated. Therefore, we ask you for the utmost confidentiality with everything we deal with in the office and we will have to investigate former employees. If anyone knows any information that can help us uncover the identity of the spy, you should meet with me. My father was the director of our company, but now I will take over the studio for the time being. Any questions?

No doubts. No one is talking. However, many whisper among themselves. Some have known each other for who knows how many years and are now beginning to suspect each other. Is this what the adult world is like? At the butcher shop, the only problem is when Dad gets excited and orders way more meat from the suppliers than he can sell. I never imagined that in the world of high business there would be spies trying to undermine fellow businessmen's businesses. That shouldn't matter to me now, though. I have to talk to Can Divit and my job hangs by a very thin thread.

After lunch, he waits for me in his office, reading reports. As I enter, he smiles at me with his usual teasing tone.

-Good afternoon, Sanem. Did you enjoy your tea? I thought it was exquisite.

-Yes, thank you very much.

My boss is still reading. I can't stand the silence. Mom always shuts up for minutes before bursting out.

-Please, Mr. Can. Don't fire me. What I said before about you and Miss Deren. I'm sorry about that. I was under a lot of stress. It's my first job... And I'm very honest. Too honest. It always brings me trouble.

-Sanem, don't worry. No one's going to fire you. I was just reading some reports for you to give to a casting agency. They're coming for it at five o'clock, so I want you to save it and give it to them. As I said, nothing should be leaked because it might give an idea of the kind of film we want to produce, so it would be best if you didn't discuss this with anyone.

-I'll deliver the folder, sir. But wouldn't it be better to send the report by e-mail?

-Yes, but I'm afraid the spy may be spying on our emails, so until this is sorted out I prefer to handle these matters the old-fashioned way.

-A very smart move-, I approve. I'm one step away from completing the image of an employee who licks the floor the boss walks on.

-Well, here you go. I don't want to keep you any longer, Sanem.

I say goodbye. On my way out, Mr. Emre calls me discreetly.

-Sanem, your work is very important, so I want you to consult with my brother and me if you have any questions about any assignment.

-Of course.

I am now the treasure keeper of the company. I take the folder and hide it in my desk. The hard part will be avoiding the gossipy Ceycey.

However, he's like a kid with a new toy talking to colleagues about the spy.

They don't bother me during the afternoon until the messenger from the casting agency arrives, so I've been practicing with the design programs on my computer. When I deliver the folder, I am notified that I must deliver others to Mr. Divit, from the casting agency and another advertising company, which stands out from the others because it is red. Apparently by this time all the mail packages arrive.

Wanting to get the packages off my hands, I place them on Can's desk and return to my workstation or, in this case, internship. I wish I could drink a little bit of tea, as the other employees always have some coffee on hand to calm my nerves. Now, however, I can no longer focus on the design. Mr. Emre approaches my desk and asks me to let him know if a red folder from an advertising company arrives.

Wow, I couldn't end my second day without another failure.

-I'm sorry. I handed the folder to his brother along with other reports.

I step back. The perfect Mr. Emre looks at me as if I've poured gasoline all over the office and then taken up smoking.

-What have you done, Sanem?! My brother must not see that folder. Get it back no matter what it takes or....

Or I'm out on my ass. That's clearer than that.

-Don't worry, sir. I'll get the folder right away.

I return to Can's office. He absentmindedly reads a black folder, thankfully. I can't figure out how to get in and get Emre's folder without him noticing, though. What's more, Can has just spotted me and frowns quizzically. Damn. I spin around. Mr. Emre finds himself like me. He's climbing the walls of his office. Eventually he's going to leave footprints on the glass. Okay, this is no time for jokes. Emre takes off his jacket. He mutters under his breath. He takes out a small red velvet box and puts it in the inside pocket of his jacket. It's a typical engagement ring box. Mr. Emre is getting married? God, this is not the time to think about that. I have to get the box back.

I try to hang around as long as possible. To disguise myself, I go to Mr. Emre to offer him coffee, but since I've been cursed I only manage to pour coffee on his suit jacket and earn an angry look from my boss.

In the end, to clean up the mess, I stay until everyone leaves the office. Can seems to amuse himself by making me suffer because he doesn't leave his office and has read all the report folders except the red one.

When he leaves his office to turn off the lights, I enter his office. However, that man is like a shadow that haunts me to torment me. When I turn around to keep watch, he appears behind me, like an apparition.

-What are you doing, Sanem?

-Excuse me, Mr. Can-, I say, putting the words together. -I was going to pick up the folders to put them away. You know. About the spy.

-Very efficient-, he compliments me. Don't worry about it. I'm going to take them home to read them there and get some work done. You should rest, though. I'll see you tomorrow.

I smile. Although all I want to do is scream my head off. I'm going to be out of a job and Mr. Emre is going to skin me after the favor he did me.

I shuffle out of the office. On the street, Emre Divit is waiting for me in a late-model Italian sports car.

-Did you get it back? -he asks me, on the verge of a nervous breakdown.

I shake my head.

-He's taking it home. He hasn't read it yet.

-You must get it back. Go into my brother's house and take it-, he says, not realizing that he's encouraging me to commit a crime.

-How? I don't even know where he lives. And if I go in and he disco-vers me...-, I try to put some sanity into it.

-No. Now I'm going to give you his address. And my brother, after returning home, goes for a run. You're going to take advantage of that moment to go in and get the folder. Here-, he says, handing me a piece of paper with his phone number on it. -I took your number from your résumé. If anything happens, call me.

After saying that, he drives off and walks away from me like I stink, or like he's running away from something.

My heart beats a mile a minute. It's moving faster than Emre's sports car and this time it's not because of my albatross' kiss.

CHAPTER V

At night I have gone out a few times with Ayhan and Leyla to some nightclub in the center of Istanbul, but I have almost always spent them in my beloved neighborhood, having dinner with my friends in one of our restaurants or walking down the street enjoying the stars. The Can Divit neighborhood, on the other hand, belonged to a completely different city. It was like entering the castle of a dark king. There were mansions with large gardens worthy of dream palaces. However, I had not gone there to enjoy the sights of a wealthy neighborhood, but to steal a folder from private property. If the police caught me, I would be the talk of the neighbors' gossip and my parents would die of a heart attack.

Mr. Emre didn't give me keys to the house, so I figure out how to sneak in. Can's house is like any of the others in the area. I don't know what I expected. At the office he was spoken of as a genius, a free spirit, and perhaps my imagination has led me to expect a quirky home, but it's average. Normal for people who accumulate millions of lira in the bank.

In the end, I decide to imitate the spies in the movie and jump over the wall, although I lack the agility and stealth of a professional thief. I almost fall on my face when I jump into Can's garden. Luckily, I brace my hands so I don't hurt myself and immediately get up. I run to the villa and enter through one of the garden entrances. Was it really that easy to sneak into a millionaire's home? There must have been some kind of trick here.

As Emre promised me, the cleaning lady has left the garden gate open and I sneak in through there. I don't know how much time I have until Can returns, so I mustn't waste too much time. I go to the living room.

I shuffle through a pile of paperwork from a desk in the dining room. There's no sign of the red folder. I approach the foyer. I see Can's jacket on a coat rack. My pulse quickens. I'm sure he'll be back any minute. He wouldn't go running all over town.

I climb the stairs and enter a room. I rummage around. I find Mr. Emre's jacket. Would this be his room when he comes to visit? My cell phone rings and I shout out of reflex.

-Hello? -I answer in a whisper.

-Sanem, did you get the folder back? -Mr. Emre blurts out. Strangely enough, he is more nervous than I am.

-No, I'm in his room. I just found his jacket.

-Yes, I tried to stay with Can and, as I had an urgent meeting, I left it there. I couldn't get the folder, but I saw how my brother left it in his study.

-Where is it?

I might be able to get out in less than five minutes.

-It's a room down the hall to the left of the kitchen. Do you know where I say?

Oh, my goodness. This house is a maze. I run to where Mr. Emre has pointed me. I jump at the glimpse of the red folder on top of a table full of photos and other papers. I grab my treasure, hoping to escape from there as soon as possible, but luck is not smiling on me. A witch must have jinxed me at birth. I hear the front door close. Mr. Can is humming a rhythmic tune and has turned on one of the stereos in the living room, because the song echoes everywhere.

I roll across the floor to hide behind a chest of drawers in the hallway and, crawling, hide in the kitchen. I am a spy. An undetectable thief. A little kitten that no one will listen to. Since Can's home is the house of a thousand doors, I flee to the living room through one of them.

-Who's there? -I hear Can say.

I have no choice. I throw the red folder at one of my boss's Chinese vases. Surely it would be from the Ching Dynasty or belong to an ancient Korean royal family. For me, however, it's the perfect basket.

-Sanem? What the hell?

Can turns on the lights. He sees me. I try to run away. Maybe if I make myself scarce he thinks I've been a hallucination. However, my boss crosses my path. We collide and he hugs me to keep me from running away. Oh, God. I smell his sweat and feel his muscles against me. It's like being trapped by a wild predator, and yet I feel safe, as if it's not the first time he's hugged me and comforted me.

-Sanem, what are you doing here?

-I...

Okay. Now he'll have to think, if I'm lucky and he doesn't call the police, that I'm a nutcase. Tomorrow I'll be fired and my mother will unhinge me with a well-deserved three-hour lecture, but I must pretend to be normal because I owe Mr. Emre a favor. A favor worth forty thousand lire. And at the thought of my other boss, my brain wakes up. I am a spy. Creating alibis is my routine, how I earn my daily bread. God, don't report me. Please, that's all I ask.

-Mr. Emre gave me the keys to his house... -, No, why? He didn't give them to me. I'm not even good at lying. -I dropped a personal item in the office when I spilled coffee on Mr. Emre's jacket. And, because your brother is such a nice person, he said he'd keep it for me while I cleaned up the mess. But... then I was embarrassed to go near him. Because his jacket is so expensive and I was afraid I'd ruined it.

Can doesn't laugh smugly. It's the first time. It would be a nice change if it weren't for the fact that he squints, hesitating whether to call the psychiatric hospital or the police.

-I don't understand anything, Sanem. What are you talking about? What does the coffee thing have to do with anything?

-It's just that Mr. Emre kept what I gave him, a very valuable gift, in his jacket and I called him because I didn't want to go home without it. I... Please... I'm so sorry.

Can twists his lips. Let him laugh. Let him think this is so funny and I'm just a lovable goofball.

-It's okay. Come with me. Don't worry about it.

I'll follow him. It's easy to keep track of him because of his manly scent. No. Focus, Sanem. It's five seconds before I announce that you don't need to come back to the office tomorrow. We enter the room where Emre's jacket is and, after a brief rummage through his pockets, he pulls out the velvet box. He opens it and we both see a ring that must cost more than a year's worth of my salary.

-Are you engaged, Sanem?

Am I engaged? Well, my friend Misifú is always going on about how we're getting married. Wait, shit.

-Yes... -I'm getting married. I'm very happy. It's a very valuable ring.

I just created a mess that I'm going to have a hard time getting out of.

-Congratulations-, Mr. Can congratulates me too formally. -Who's the lucky guy?

-My boyfriend? -Obviously. I wasn't going to marry my father. -This... a friend of the family.

In my mind an image materializes of me, dressed as a bride, in front of the altar, about to kiss Misifú. I almost faint and Mr. Can threatens to hug me again to hold me.

-I'm leaving. Please don't send me away.

I am not a spy. Abort mission. We have to get out of here as soon as possible.

-Of course I won't fire you, Sanem. -Where are you going?

To my home, to the cozy wall around Can's house. To freedom. Away from my handsome boss. No, Sanem. Clear mind. Let's pretend to be normal.

Unfortunately, I know that when I think coldly about what happened tonight, I'll want to smother myself with my pillow. I run away from Mr. Can, who keeps calling me, and instead of going out the door like a normal person, I jump over the garden wall and this time I really hurt myself when I fall.

Mr. Can comes out of his house through the front door. He is majestic, like a king coming out of his castle to mingle with the populace. I, on the other hand, find myself lying on the sidewalk with my pants torn, stained with blood, and a wound on my leg.

-Sanem, come in, please-, his majesty invites me as a work of charity.

-No need, sir-, his faithful commoner replies. -I'll call for a carriage... I mean, a cab.

I limp away, without dignity, because the villagers who dare to speak to the king cannot hope to get away with anything.

I stop at a bus stop. I look at my wound. It's not serious, but it's not superficial either, and if my mother catches me on my way home, she'll ask for explanations and I can't think of what excuse to make. I've run out of imagination with Can. Tomorrow I won't dare look him in the face and it will be worse when I meet Mr. Emre. In fact, I should call him now to explain what happened.

I type on my phone, reminiscing about my excursion to Can's chalet. I immediately wander and fantasize about Can's scent. His embrace. I return to a darkened room, where my albatross pulls me close to him as he kisses me. I shake my head. I'm starting to lose my mind. I need to unveil the true identity of my albatross and stop associating my boss with him because he has a beard and is just as muscular.

I focus on Emre's voice, demanding that I tell him everything.

-The folder is still at his brother's house.

-But, Sanem!!!! -he shouts, instantly clearing my head.

-Listen to me, Mr. Emre. I hid it so your brother won't find it. Unless he's cleaning up in the middle of the night. Which, knowing Mr. Can...

Sanem, this is not the time to be funny.

-Where did you leave it?

-In a black vase in the living room. It's Chinese, Korean. Well, I don't know what it is, but it's easy to find.

I listen to how my boss controls his breathing. There is a mystery behind this matter.

-Why is the folder so important, Mr. Emre? I don't understand why I had to sneak into your brother's house.

Quiet. Maybe I've been meddling where I'm not wanted.

-What I'm about to tell you, Sanem, you can't tell anyone. Especially my brother. The future of my father's studio and business depends on it.

I swallow. Now he's going to confess to me that Mr. Can is involved in drug trafficking.

-I think the spy in the studio is my brother. He doesn't get along with my father and wants to get rid of the company. The leak didn't work for him, so now he's trying to sell the company to the competition and get our father out of management. The folder you gave him is a secret project of mine to try to get him out of management.

I can't believe my ears. How can you be so devious? Mr. Can is trying to pretend he doesn't care about anything, with his bohemian artist airs, and behind his back he is only trying to bring down his family. Poor Mr. Emre. I remember when I was with his father at the hotel and he was worried about him.

-Sanem, I regret having brought you into this, but without your help I will not be able to thwart my brother's plot.

-Sir, I don't know how to help you. I am just a humble, inexperienced designer.

-Therein lies your chief virtue. My brother will not suspect you. He's overconfident because he now runs the studio as he pleases.

That's true. Can is a conceited guy and that's why it didn't even cross his mind that I made up a story and he didn't rule out that I was a lost idiot. Okay, there the situation didn't leave me in good stead. However, a shiver runs through my skin. I could show my talent and thank Mr. Emre for the favor.

-You can trust me. I will do whatever you ask me to do.

The bus approaches. My leg still hurts, but it's a small thing compared to what's coming.

-We'll talk tomorrow at the office. Thank you very much, Sanem.

CHAPTER VI

Today in the studio they are going to do a casting with the actors they have brought from the agency and Mr. Can has decided that the best thing to do was to create a relaxed atmosphere. He has decided that, after the auditions, we will all go to his house to celebrate a small party. That way, the actors could get acquainted with the studio and make more contacts, since Can has also invited some of his acquaintances from the world.

I look at my boss. The corrupt one. Mr. Emre is talking to some producers and has invited them over for a glass of wine. We've barely spoken this morning, but he's asked me to photograph the secret projects Can asks me to guard so we can get a head start on the man who enjoys attracting the gazes of aspiring young superstars. In fact, I think some of the girls who make Can's eyes fall out have already been on TV starring in soap operas.

I still find it hard to believe what Mr. Emre told me last night, but it fits with what always happens. In the end, the pretty boys are always the bad guys. Besides, Can had already shown me his superiority. I'm sure he thought he had the upper hand. However, I'll put everything on the line to repay Emre's trust in me.

Deren has asked me to keep up appearances and not to talk to anyone unless I am asked for a drink or a favor of any kind. Ceycey has told me to enjoy myself and he and Güliz are interested in my leg wound. Since I'm wearing a short skirt, I can't hide last night's mess. The best thing would have been to wear long pants, but the company is very strict about etiquette and Deren is obsessed with appearance. Besides, my knee is stinging.

The only good thing is that there is a barbecue. The smell of grilled meat gets my taste buds tingling. I'm glad the actresses don't usually eat much to keep in shape, since we play to more for the others. I approach Mr. Can, who is cooking while talking to Deren and two gentlemen. He is the perfect host.

-Good morning, Sanem. Here we go again.

Hungry. The grilled meat is juicy. I must appear normal. Otherwise I'll lose my sandwich.

- Is the meat a long way from being ready?

It's a prime steak. Growing up with a butcher has made me an expert on the subject.

-Eating meat is vulgar-, says the ignorant Deren. -Let's cook vegetable skewers. We must think of our guests.

-Most of my guests prefer a vegetarian diet, so I don't know what to do with this," says Can without paying attention to her.

-I wouldn't mind making myself a sandwich.

Fortune is making up for last night.

-Well, since the meat is ready, I'm going to fix you lunch. You look hungry.

Deren makes a notch of disgust, as if I were a drooling puppy looking for leftovers. However, when Can offers me a delicious-looking sandwich, I smile at him with the happiness that comes from the first bite.

-Do you want another sandwich?

-No, two is too much for me.

It's one thing to have good taste and another to get carried away by gluttony, especially since I'm afraid Deren will catch my eye later.

-Well, the other sandwich will be for me-, Can says, eating the other one and winking at me. It's a pity he's such a trickster. I almost think he likes me.

I walk away from the barbecue. I don't feel like listening to Deren's mutterings. She's very talkative today, especially to Can. I guess nastiness attracts. I devour my sandwich and stroll to the poolside. I wish I could take a dip.

-Good morning, Sanem-, Mr. Emre greets me. -Thank you for last night. I retrieved the folder and talked to my brother to keep your alibi.

My head keeps fantasizing about the taste of meat. But now, I start to think about what happened last night and I realize that Mr. Emre is watching me without saying anything. I think I'm forgetting something, although I can't figure out what it is I'm overlooking.

-I think it would be best for you to keep your fake engagement for a while and keep wearing the ring until then.

I feel like I've eaten a sandwich of rocks. The pressure in my stomach makes me stagger.

-No, Mr. Emre. It's a very expensive ring. I carry it in my purse and...

I rush to him to return the ring. How could I have forgotten that? However, I am clumsiness personified and as I leave, I slip on a puddle and fall into the pool as I wished, although I never imagined it would be like this.

Emre holds out a hand to me, worried. I'm sure he regrets entrusting me with such an important mission as being Can's spy.

-Breathe, Sanem. It's nothing-, my boss reassures me. -It's just a ring and if you wear it on your finger you can't possibly lose it.

Sure, as if I could wear a piece of jewelry like that in my neighborhood without arousing suspicion, especially from my mother.

-Sir, I...

-Come on, get out of the pool, Sanem.

Emre pulls me and I come out dripping. What an image I make. Deren is going to rip my skin to shreds.

-Now, you're going to my room. Where my jacket was yesterday. There's a dryer and you can use spare clothes of mine.

How can he be so different from his brother?

-When you're done-, Emre continues, -you get dressed and put on your ring so as not to arouse my brother's suspicions. I'll leave your bag in the living room. I'll ask Ceycey for it.

I nod in despair. My clumsiness is going to be known throughout the office.

I walk back into the palace of Can Divit. At this rate, I'm going to know every nook and cranny. I go upstairs and take refuge in Mr. Emre's room. I see the dryer, although it seems to me that the room is a little different. There are books in every corner. In the end, I shrug my shoulders. Last night I explored in the dark. I strip down to just my underwear and put my dress in the dryer. I open a closet and put on a white sport shirt that fits me like a dress. While I wait, I gossip through Emre's books. There are many volumes of art, poetry and novels from all eras. I recognize many classics. I am surprised that, being so cultured, Emre is so humble. He and Can are like night and day.

I smile to see that Mr. Emre reads many of my favorite poets.

-What are you doing in my room, Sanem? -Can says behind me.

My heart stops. I'm half naked in front of my boss. In his room. Slowly, I turn around and almost faint. Can is wearing only a towel and pants. His herculean chest looks free. Today he smells like barbecue. The meat that makes me salivate... Sanem, focus. That man is a scoundrel who wants to sink his family business.

-I... fell into the pool, sir... -Your brother told me to go into his room to use the dryer.

-Did he offer you my room?

-No, his. Mr. Emre's, I mean. But I got lost and...

Can laughs at me. I'm thankful he's not a slimeball and doesn't look me up and down. I'm the one who runs over every inch of skin with his gaze. I'm about to be dismissed....

-Sir, please. Turn around. This situation may degenerate into harassment at work and I don't want...

-Sanem, this is the second time you've entered my house without my permission. Does the concept of breaking and entering ring a bell?-, he asks me in a cocky tone, although he has turned around. -I don't know how you manage to end up like this. I hope it doesn't become a habit. What would your fiancé say if he saw you like this?

Damn him.

-Trust prevails in our relationship. We love each other madly-, I blurt out. I wish I knew my albatross so I could talk about him like that.

-And why aren't you wearing his ring?

-It's just that... I still can't get used to the idea of wearing such an expensive piece of jewelry. I'm from a poor neighborhood, Mr. Can. You wouldn't understand.

-You can call me by my first name, Sanem. With what has happened in the last two days, formalities are superfluous, so may I offer to heal your wound? I'll bet twenty lira you haven't disinfected it.

On the one hand, it would do me good to clean my knee and pour some hydrogen peroxide on it. On the other, I didn't feel like giving Can the courtesy of taking care of me. He wasn't a good man, just a damned attractive one who knew how to choose the right words to seduce his victims.

-It's nothing. Besides, I don't want to be a bother.

-It's no trouble, woman. In my travels I've often had to heal myself. When you go out into nature, you can only depend on yourself.

Ever since I was a child, the image I had formed of executives was of individuals in suits who mercilessly exploited their employees in exchange for a small handout. Can, however, tenderly instructs me to put on a pair of sweatpants while he reaches for a T-shirt. He then sits me down in a soft armchair and disinfects my wound with tremendous gentleness. As he wipes a cotton swab with hydrogen peroxide, my skin shivers and I hold my breath. After applying a band-aid and smiling at me, I have to remind myself that this man is a first-rate actor. He doesn't care about me. If he was capable of ruining his family, why should he care about me?

-How are you?-, he asks without a hint of mockery, and his image becomes again that of a magnanimous king looking after his servants. His voice melts my heart and I am aware that it is not the first time it happens, although I can't remember when he seduced me for the first time.

-Thank you very much, Can-, I say, forgetting that he is my boss and that our relationship should be strictly business.

He accompanies me back to the garden. Fortunately, Deren is not feeling well. Ceycey and Güliz accompany her and offer her a glass of water. It's lucky because if she catches me leaving the chalet in Can's company, I'd get a good one.

During the rest of the party, I pay attention to my fellow company members. There are several of them with beards. I imagine myself in the arms of one of them. It doesn't work out. Only Can appears to me because of last night. Damn, I would have to go one by one, meet them and then I would recognize my albatross. But what if my mysterious gentleman was just a fantasy? Can was the example that men could pretend before others, offer a face of generosity and kindness when the reality was quite different.

-Deren has had a little too much to drink. You should have seen her talking to Mr. Can-, Güliz tells me. I didn't notice that she approached me and offered me a glass of wine.

I drink. I have to keep a cool head. Forget about him.

-I'm glad. It would have been awkward to laugh in front of her.

-Don't believe that. This one won't remember a thing. And thank goodness, because I guess she'd take her frustration out on us. Hey, Sanem. Are you okay?

I need to talk to someone. Ayhan is a good confidant, but Guliz can help me find him.

-Do you know all the employees at the studio?

-Well, not all of them. By name I do, although I know most of the gossip because people come to me for advice. Do you want to open your heart to me, Sanem? -she asks me with a mischievous smile.

-Yes, I'm looking for my albatross.

-Who is it?

-I don't know who he is. That's why I call him that. It's a man who kissed me at the company party.

And without further ado, I proceed to tell her about the magical encounter of that night...

CHAPTER VII

I told my story to Güliz and Ayhan later when I got off work. We met after work for dinner at a restaurant in the harbor. They both decided to call my romantic stranger albatross. It's become our code name, so Güliz is going to prepare a list of partners who could be my man and now I'm looking at pictures of the studio employees.

-This is Ceycey-, I say, showing him his Instagram.

-He looks really nice-, Ayhan comments.

-He's a sweetheart.

-Hey, what about Mr. Can? I heard he's a very famous person. I heard it at the hair salon.

I look for Can's Instagram. I find pictures of him in nature, war scenes, we see awareness messages and at the end we find a picture where he is bathing in a river bare-chested, like a Greek god.

-Oh, sir. I'm drooling.

I don't know what to say. I would like to tell him that all that glitters is not gold. Still, Can seems like a committed person. He took the refugee photos in person and as a protest image. He has seen the world. He cares about others when he's so rich he could live from party to party without a care in the world.

-So who do you think your albatross is?-, Ayhan asks me. -It could be Can. He has a beard and if he catches me with those arms, I'd melt all over.

No. It can't be him. Because he's so handsome, my head plays tricks on me, but Emre has already shown me his brother's true character.

When we get home, Leyla talks to my mother, sitting on the couch in front of the TV. My sister wipes away an indiscreet tear. I have always admired Leyla even though my parents constantly compare me to her. Nothing discourages her. She has resources for everything.

-Sanem, Misifú's family is coming for dinner-, Mom says, changing the subject. She manages to get a smile out of Leyla's face.

-Dinner? What do they want?-, I ask, although I can't imagine anything good.

-Remember we told you that you might have to marry Misifú if you didn't get a job?

No. That was a crude ploy to get me to hurry up and send resumes to every company in Istanbul. They couldn't have said anything to Misifu. Ever since we were kids he took any smile as a sign that she was madly in love with him. If my mother ever hinted to him that they were ready to give our marriage a blessing, she would rush to arrange our honeymoon and find school for the children.

-Mom. I can't marry Misifu. It's... it's... it's Misifu!!!!

-Poor Muzaffer. You're going to break his heart-, Leyla said viciously.

-Nothing is going to happen. You know his mother wants to arrange the marriage and Misifu is very enthusiastic.

-I'm not going to indulge his fantasies, Mom. He's obsessed with me!

-They are family friends-, my mother interjects again. I know that although she seems like a reasonable person now, if I insist that she doesn't want to add fuel to Misifú's uncontrolled love, Mom will bring out her dictatorial housewife character. -It will be a nice dinner and you can talk. And if you don't want to marry him...

-I tell him, of course. As if that would work.

I have been insisting to Misifu for I don't know how many years that I would never fall in love with him, even though he must speak a special dialect of Turkish because he has never understood me.

I go to bed. Even though I have a dinner with Misifu waiting for me, I think about Leyla. What happened to her? Mom told me about the dinner because she wanted to change the subject. If I think about it, I haven't known my sister's secrets for years. She tells everything to my mother. Instead, I accumulate more and more secrets. First I have paid the forty thousand lire of debt thanks to a favor from my boss and then I have become a kind of spy inside my company. Too many secrets in three days and that's not counting my albatross. What will I do when I find him? What will I tell him? Did he dream about me or was it just a mistake and that kiss of love was not meant for me?

I look at the books in my room. Some titles were also in Can's room. I think of my boss, the man with two faces. On the one hand, the bohemian artist who travels the world and who, instead of living in a bubble, cares for the underprivileged. On the other, the man who plans to destroy his family, I suppose out of selfishness. However, if there is one thing we both share, it is a love for books because I, as much as I dream of being a writer, have not yet dared to do more than scribble a few notebooks. I pick one up and reread old sketches of novels. I'm not like Can, he creates. He photographs beautiful landscapes and right now he's producing a film that fills him with emotion. And me? Maybe I should write about my albatross. He is worthy of a fantasy novel, of great romances. Maybe my feelings will make it easier for the letters to flow. I pick up a pen and suck on the tip. I begin to write a novel:

"I have two dreams in life. The first, to be a great writer and the second, to live in the Galapagos; where are they? only the one who goes there knows. The Galapagos Islands, the place where I want to spend the rest of my life. It may sound crazy, but what's wrong with dreaming? It helps you escape from the harsh reality, the harsh reality...".

I reread the first paragraph. It is curious. For the first time, I feel like continuing the story to the end, printing it out and binding it to be read, especially by my dear albatross. First, however, I must find it, find it among the faces of my co-workers. On the outside they are ordinary men, although, like Can, my albatross will have two faces and the real one will be wonderful.

The next morning, I talk to Güliz and Ceycey. Our mission: to locate the albatross. We draw up a list of names and I start crossing them off until the reunion takes place.

Deren is not shouting orders at us today. The effects of the hangover will still be with her. Can calls me and tells me to come with him.

-Today we have to go to a printer. We have to print the script of the film and a couple of promotional images. With them, you'll make your first design. What's that in your hand?

With no respect for my privacy, he gets the list, headed with the title Operation Albatross: men with beards. Yes, we are not the height of creativity.

-This...-, Sometimes it's easier to tell the truth. -I'm looking for a man I met at my first day party. He had a beard.

-And what does your fiancé think of that? You're not wearing your ring today either.

Reluctantly, I put it on to shut him up.

-I told you I don't like to draw attention to myself and this is not what you think.

-And why am I not here? I was at the party. In fact, I invited you and I have a beard-, he points with his Machiavellian smile. I hate this man.

-No, it's not you I'm looking for, Mr. Can.

-You're still not on a first-name basis-, my boss insists. -That's all right. We're in a hurry. Let's go to my car.

He quickens his pace and I run after him like a lapdog. I attract stares as I leave with the boss, especially Deren, who judges me mercilessly. What does she want me to do? Can is the big boss. If he orders me to do something, I must obey.

-Can, wait. I want to talk to Sanem for a moment-, Emre interrupts us.

We pull back a little. Emre hurries to whisper instructions in my ear. Today is another one of my days as a spy.

-Take a picture of Can's script and send it to me. I don't know what he's up to.

-Okay, sir.

Then I follow Mr. Can, who's waiting for me in an SUV that I'm sure has been to the most inhospitable places on the planet.

-Maybe our working day will be a little longer. Do you mind?-, Can asks me, with his hands on the steering wheel.

-Not at all.

My mission is to expose him. I don't care how long it takes.

Can drives through the streets of Istanbul, through a neighborhood I've never been to before. He plays music on the radio, although I think he's waiting for me to open a conversation. What can I say that he finds interesting, though?

-You are an interesting girl, Sanem.

How you can intimidate me with such a simple phrase is beyond me.

-What do you mean?

-Well, I remember your interview. You have a great design sensibility, you're funny and with you I have no problem finding a restaurant. We'll have lunch together today. Do you want to go somewhere special?

-What do you mean you have no problem finding a restaurant with me?-, I ask, fearing that the sly comment is coming soon.

-I don't know if you've noticed, but everyone in the office is obsessed with diets and refined dishes. They don't even appreciate a good Turkish tea like we do.

I was wrong. So far he behaves like a decent human being. He's not a snob.

-I like to eat. Besides, if you're talking about the barbecue, my parents own a butcher shop. If I didn't like a good steak, it would mean I was adopted.

-A real girl. It's hard to find someone like you when you surround yourself with actresses and super models. The world I move in is too superficial. That's why I like to travel to places where I can have a clash with reality. If I'm honest, Istanbul suffocates me. If I stay here, it's because of my father.

No. It's impossible to spy on this man. It completely throws me off. Doctor Jeckyll and Mr. Hyde, although if I'm honest, he's never treated me badly.

I am not asking about Mr. Divit. Can doesn't seem to want to pursue the matter. Perhaps his relationship with his family is more complex than I imagined, although Mr. Emre has shown me his darker side. I wish I could ask him why he wants to sink the family business. Does he wish he could run far away from here and get lost in a city at war or on a mountain in the middle of the desert?

-Here is the printing press, Sanem. They are friends of my father's and our companies have collaborated together on many occasions. They will probably take us into their confidence, so don't listen to them.

The print shop is a neat and simple building. Surely the Divits' studio could afford the services of a larger firm, so if they work here, it's because they really are friends of the family.

The business owner hugs Can and asks him about his travels. They lose themselves for a few minutes in anecdotes that don't concern me, although, without my noticing, they bring me into the conversation.

-Be careful with this man, daughter. He's a free spirit. At the slightest distraction he'll be gone with the wind.

-Don't frighten my employees, Sahim.

Can hands them a folder and asks for fifty copies. Then he says goodbye and invites me to lunch. I accept with my mind in rapt attention because my brain is working on a method to photograph the script and send it to Emre.

-Even though you're a meat fanatic, today I'm in the mood for fish and a nice salad.

-That's fine with me, Can-, I reply, my brain cells smoking.

My boss smiles, not smug, just happy.

-Is something wrong?

-You've stopped calling me by my first name. You don't see me as your superior's ogre anymore?

-You've never been an ogre-, I reply. I'm more comfortable with the informality. -You and Emre have been very good to me. In fact, I find it strange.

It sure does. Deren for example never calls me by my name. Sometimes I get used to it and sometimes my blood boils with rage.

-I understand you. When I was a student and went to an internship company, I was treated like a slave. I was the coffee boy and, deep down, I didn't do too badly because of my father. Everyone wants to win his approval, so they weren't too strict with me, although that didn't stop me from seeing how my colleagues were treated. Since then, I decided to dedicate myself to my dream and be, as Sahim has rightly defined me, a free spirit.

I start to get interested in his life, in what he has encountered outside Turkey. He tells me about his early years as an artistic photographer. Can takes me to a restaurant in the harbor, one where I would never have set foot on my own, but he invites me and recommends the specialty on the menu.

-What is your dream, Sanem? I can't imagine you working for life in our studio. You're a dreamy girl.

When had we started talking about me? I wasn't as interesting as he was. I had only written a few short stories in my teens and last night a sketch about a novel that was more like an artistic autobiography.

-I want to be a writer. Although I am aware that it is a dream that is hard to make come true. I'd rather have a steady income to help my family.

-The butcher's shop, right? What's it called?

I smile. As a child, that story had always seemed beautiful to me, although it also made me a little envious.

-Butcher Leyla, like my sister. My parents met at a party-, I say, thinking of the first encounter with my albatross. -Dancing to the song Leyla. Then when they got married and opened the butcher shop they named it Leyla. It was their talisman and, when my sister was born, they gave her the same name.

-You come from a family of dreamers-, Can points out without mocking. There was respect in those eyes that were trying to bore into mine and took my breath away. -A writer daughter is the least they could expect.

It was true, what he meant about my parents. Dad and Mom often argue over silly things, but they love each other madly and know how to touch each other's hearts with a few words.

-If we're successful with this project, maybe you can be encouraged to send us scripts. Who knows? Maybe I have the new Turkish break-through artist in front of me.

I blush. No one has ever had such confidence in my talent, except for my friend Ayhan. Mom insists that I put my feet on the ground and look for a job where I can make a living. That's why she threatened me to marry Misifu. It's not like we're still living in the 16th century.

-Thank you very much, Can-, I confess.

Why do all the handsome and charming men actually hide a horrible personality? However, I feel grateful for your words. They are not mere politeness. For a moment, I feel like he understands me. I'm sure his parents didn't approve of him going halfway around the world with only a camera.

-What kind of world do we live in?-, he points to himself.

During the rest of the meal, he recommends a novel he is reading about immigrants forced into exile. Thanks to the interesting subject matter, I forget my headaches and we return to the printer's office engaged in a conversation about why so many successful artists take so little interest in the miseries of their fellow human beings. Next to me is no longer a gallant man with bohemian artist's pretensions, but a sensitive man who knows how to look beyond what meets the eye.

-Good afternoon, Sahim, is our order ready?

The owner of the printing house is sweating profusely.

-I'm sorry, Can. There are problems with the electrical installation. We won't be able to fix it until tomorrow.

Can mumbles under his breath.

-With one more day, we wouldn't have had any trouble getting your order to you on time.

-It's not your fault, Sahim. Because of leakage problems, I had decided to print this on the last day to keep copies of the project at home.

-Maybe you can order it from another printer.

-At this hour it's impossible-, Can replies, although he frowns in concentration. -Do you still keep the manual printer?

-Sure, it's a gem, but I don't think it's any good to you.

-Of course I do. They used to produce wonders.

They disagree for several minutes, but in the end Can manages to convince Sahim. They lead us to a storage room where the printing press is located. I look at it in ecstasy. That device must be older than my parents put together.

-Do you like it?-, Can asks me with a smile.

I nod like a child at a birthday present.

-We're going to make two copies to show at tomorrow's meeting with the producers-, Can tells me. Tomorrow we'll print the rest.

Then, with infinite patience and gentleness, Can explains to me how the printing press works and the placement of the iron plates and paper. After half an hour, my hands are dripping with ink, although I laugh with my boss as if we were in the middle of a school assignment and then recess awaits.

-What's the movie about?

-It's a love story. It always works, although as a good writer you know that the importance lies in the details. The script is written by a friend and me, but hopefully you'll write the next one.

I blush again, embarrassed. I have to remind myself that manipulators deceive their victims by creating another face with which they can break through any wall. However, a part of me believes in Can. Was it that simple? After what Mr. Emre had revealed to me?

The last thing we printed was the logo for the film. A very simple design of a dolphin.

-I want you to improve this later, but it will do for now. I'm going to talk to Sahim. Can you keep the copies in two folders?

-Of course.

Left alone, I organize the sheets and take out my cell phone. I start photographing the script sheets one by one, although since I didn't know how much time I had and didn't want Can to catch me like the times I snuck into his house, I focus on the first few pages, the logo and the main plot summary. With the files in my possession, I quickly send them to Mr. Emre.

I breathe a little easier despite the pressure in my stomach.

When Can returns, he doesn't suspect a thing and we say goodbye to Sahim. My boss insists on accompanying me home, although I won't even let him leave me at the door. The neighbors would make a thousand and one movies about us, especially Misifu, and with so much stress the last thing I wanted to do was listen to him.

I say goodbye to my boss on a street that borders the neighborhood. Can bids me good night and I smile like a schoolgirl. I say goodbye to him. I listen as his car drives away. I imagine him as a giant albatross lost at sea until he returns again to the Galapagos.

I sigh. It's about time I stopped associating my boss with the albatross. Firstly, because he only saw me as an employee and, secondly, because I wanted my love to flow only to the stranger who kissed me at the party. Undoubtedly, that man was not Can.

He couldn't be.

CHAPTER VIII

Ayhan called me at eleven o'clock at night after melting my cell phone with her messages. Leyla and mom are chatting in the kitchen, so I tip-toed to my room.

-What's new in Operation Albatross?-, my friend asks with an evil chuckle. -You're home late from work, any attractive men entertaining you on the way out?

-I hope so-, I laugh as I realize who I'm back with. -Mr. Can and I were printing an important report. The printer had a setback and I had to work overtime. At least my boss promised to pay me at the end of the month.

-Oh, sir! You spent a whole afternoon with Can Divit! Alone?

-Yes, but not...

-Something happened! I want all the details, Sanem!

I throw myself on the bed and bounce on the mattress like a sack of potatoes. I'm so exhausted I almost feel like one.

-Actually, I've been accompanying him on his errands all day. We talked quite a bit in the car and at lunch, and on the outside, he's a fascinating man.

-Oh, Sanem, are you going to dare to put a stop to this gift of nature?

-It's just that his brother confessed a secret plan of Can's to me. I'm not supposed to tell anyone, it's just that...

-Let's see. How long have we known each other? -Ayhan asks me. As I think about the answer, I discover that my friend has been with me for as long as I can remember.

-For as long as I can remember?

-That's right. We are like sisters. You've told me everything. More than sisters, the two of us are a part of each other, so if you tell me something it's like you're reflecting out loud.

I smile. I'd love to hug Ayhan right now.

-Okay. Listen carefully. It's important that you don't interrupt me.

I explain in detail the mess of the folders and my mission to infiltrate Can's villa, including the disastrous outcome and the problem with the ring. I also tell him about my conversation with Mr. Emre at the barbecue and, finally, about the spying I did at the printer's today. By the end, my tongue is parched, but I've let it all out and enjoy the relaxation while waiting for Ayhan to give me his opinion.

-Let me get this straight, that Greek god hugged you after you went for a run and you rubbed up against him and the next day you sneak half-naked into his room and find him shirtless about to take a shower?

The one who needs a cold shower right now is Ayhan.

-Are you really just looking at that?

-Well, there have always been business disputes and if I were you, I'd stay out of them.

-Mr. Emre paid me forty thousand liras and with that money I saved the butcher's shop. I must be grateful.

-Okay, you've convinced me. However, I don't think Mr. Can is so bad.

-You're not thinking with your head-, I reproach her.

-No, I'm telling you, not with my head...

-Ayhan!

We both burst out laughing like little girls. I can never be thankful enough for the good fortune of having Ayhan as a friend.

-What I've told you. You're in the middle of a Divit problem. Stay out of it within your means and, in the meantime, enjoy the view. Let me know tomorrow how operation albatross is progressing.

We hang up. If only it were that easy to forget that Can is cheating on his family. Leyla and I argue often, although I would never think of betraying her. My workday has been so long that today I don't fall asleep fantasizing about the albatross, but thinking about Can.

The next morning, I am surprised to go downstairs for breakfast and find Leyla and Mom in the kitchen. My sister always gets up like the chickens and goes to work well in advance so as not to be late.

-Is it your day off?

I yawn like the biggest lion on the savannah and open the fridge. Inside is a big jug of milk, so I take it out and make myself a cocoa.

-You're a busybody, Sanem.

Said the frying pan to the saucepan. Sometimes she sounds like my second mother because of the questions she asks me about my private life.

-Your sister has taken a week off from work.

I look at Leyla. I don't buy that lie. I'm the queen of excuses and that one is too pathetic. My sister dodges my scrutinizing gaze. Her eyes are bloodshot and a little shiny. I'm afraid she's crying again.

-Leyla is the hardest working person in the world. I can't believe she took a week off voluntarily.

Mom comforts Leyla. The poor thing is hyperventilating. She should blow off some steam. We're sisters and everyone knows I'm the dumb one in the family.

-The Divit's company has suffered leaks and one happened on a project I was involved in, so my agency is analyzing my computer to see if I sent an email to a competing agency.

-No!-, I snap indignantly. -That's stupid! I'll talk to Mr. Can tomorrow. I'm his personal assistant and I won't leave him alone until he believes in your innocence.

-Are you Mr. Can's personal assistant?-, Mom is surprised.

-Yes, until they give me design work. I also know Mr. Emre. In fact, I have his number. I'm going to call him. Weren't you his consultant, Leyla?

-Sanem, no!-, she interrupts me when she sees me pull out my cell phone and realizes I'm not bluffing. -I appreciate the gesture, but I don't want to be embarrassed anymore. I'm innocent, so I just have to wait for my computer to be analyzed. Besides, if you intercede on my behalf, maybe they'll investigate you too.

My sister smiled at me, although I notice that it's hard for her, so I give her a hug. I know deep down she likes them, and she hugs me back. In the end, Mom hugs both of us too.

-I'm so proud that you take care of each other. My two little girls.

Family is the most important treasure. As I say goodbye to Leyla, that certainty guides my steps to work. I have seen a hint of pride in my older sister's eyes. She has always been scolding and advising me. However, today I have been the one taking care of her and I will continue to do so, so, despite what Leyla says, I will talk to Mr. Emre. If I explain the situation to him, he will understand. My boss is one of the most understanding and generous men I have ever met. He will be able to intercede for Leyla at his company.

In the office, Ceycey and Güliz rush at me to find out yesterday's details. I live surrounded by wives, although there's not much to tell. I don't plan to tell anything about my conversation with Can. The only one I can calmly unburden myself to is Ayhan, since she knows me and is aware of what it means that Can has supported me in my dream of becoming a writer.

-That's Ahmed-, Güliz points out to me. -Ahmed is a bearded midd-le-aged man. Is he your albatross?

No way. I called my stranger an albatross because he's powerful and Ahmed is starting to suffer the effects of the beer in his belly.

-Girls, Deren is coming-, Ceycey warns us.

Our boss comes in like a bulldog and looks at me like I'm a stray cat.

-Mr. Can is going to announce the new project. This morning the producers gave him the go-ahead on the final version of the script.

The colleagues are talking excitedly about the film we are going to shoot and, to be honest, excitement is running through my body as well. Can will soon commission my first design and, when it's finished, I'll run to show it to mom and Leyla.

We reconvene in the boardroom and Can is standing on a chair recei-ving the applause of his employees. He is elated. Next to him, Mr. Emre looks crestfallen and a doubt assails me. Did I make a mistake yesterday?

We have a title and a budget for the film, all we need to do is get the hottest actress in Turkey and our studio will rise to the top!-, says Can. -Comrades, I present to you the early version of our first film: The Vo-yage of the Albatross.

I am stunned. Ceycey and Güliz hold me.

-Are you all right, Sanem? -They ask me.

I can't believe it. Is it a coincidence or did I inspire Mr. Can yesterday? Me! The most mediocre girl he will ever meet!

Amidst the cheers, Can winks at me. Okay, I'm not dreaming. I don't know what to expect from that man. As the crowd disperses, back to their desks, Mr. Emre approaches me.

-Sir, I'm sorry....

Emre doesn't scold me. He smiles at me in consolation.

-Don't apologize, Sanem. You did a great job. Unfortunately, my brother outsmarted us and what you printed yesterday was a decoy. Apparently, in the evening he went back to the printer and printed another version. I guess he had one of his outbursts of inspiration. He is unpredictable.

He changed the script for me. It's inexplicable, but yesterday we talked about the albatross and suddenly he comes up with this new version. The man is having fun playing with me.

-But we can still thwart his plans, Sanem-, Emre whispers to me. -Can is meeting with the actress of the moment. Take it upon yourself to sabotage the meeting. And don't be afraid to wear the ring, Sanem-, he whispers, a little amused. -If you take it off and put it on all the time, Can will get suspicious and bombard you with questions.

Emre knows his brother well. He is a master in the art of baffling his victims. Can approaches me. Today he is not dressed in comfortable clothes, but in explorer's attire. Comfortable boots, jacket and casual pants to match.

-What do you think of the title?-, he says to me as if it's nothing. Emre gives us space. Before Can says anything, I put on my ring. He notices the gesture, but doesn't comment.

-It's... interesting.

-How modest you are. The albatross is the symbol of Baudelaire's poem, the man who loves for life, the poet who returns home to know love. Why are you looking for an albatross?

-It's a stupid nickname, Mr. Can. I am like that.

-That's why you're so special, Sanem-, he says, throwing me off balance. -If you don't mind. I want you to come with me today, too. I'm meeting with actress Arzu Tas. I want to convince her to act in our film and I could use an assistant.

-Where are we going?

-To Amasra. We have quite a long trip ahead of us, so get ready. We're leaving now.

Can must have had three pots of coffee instead of his cup of tea because he's going like a formula one. He could make it to Amasra without a car. In the middle of the garage he stops and thinks. We are going to travel in a company car. It's not his SUV, but a five-year-old car. The greedy could have bought a better one.

-I left my wallet in the office.

-I'll get it-, I reassure him, even though my boss is now the reincarnation of the roadrunner and can't sit still for five minutes.

-It doesn't matter. Do you know how to drive?

-Yes, but...

-Perfect. You'll take us to Amasra.

It's been a year since I got my license and Leyla lets me borrow her car from time to time, so I'm not too happy about a long trip. We can get stranded in the middle of the road. Can tunes the radio to a station with the latest hits and I smile at the plan I just came up with.

I wait until I leave Istanbul because I don't want to get home with a fine, and on the highway I drive at the minimum speed allowed. Can, who until then had been pensive, starts muttering and encourages me to go faster.

-I'm sorry. I haven't had my license for long-, I apologized, feigning seriousness.

That placated Can. At least he wasn't saying anything else to me even though I had formed a small traffic jam and cars were passing me at every opportunity. Although it was obvious that I was about to give him a heart attack.

-Sanem, you're going to ruin the engine if you brake like that-, he said with good reason. As I am not an experienced driver, I sometimes make mistakes, and my driving school teacher warned me that I was braking too sharply.

-What do you say? This car is too old. They could have replaced it.

Can bites his nails and puts his hands in his pocket. He hears the sound of stones clattering and the sound that soothes my boss is unnerving to me. The radio prevents silence between us. Can watches in the rearview mirror the line of cars that has formed behind us.

So much silence attacks my nerves and I consider speeding up because Amasra is far away and I don't want to get home too late. However, a firecracker startles me.

-Go to the platform, Sanem-, Can advises me in a calm voice, although his expression is nervous.

I park there. Next to us the cars start to accelerate and, little by little, the traffic jam disappears.

Can gets out of the car and kneels down next to a tire.

-We have a flat tire-, he informs me.

-It wasn't my fault.

I don't know if I've convinced him, but he takes off his jacket and goes to the trunk. He pulls out a spare tire and a toolbox.

-You'll have to give me a hand, Sanem.

I nod. Can holds out the toolbox. First I hand him a jack and then he changes the wheel with my help. We both end up with our hands stained with dirt and grease, although my boss gets the worst of it.

-I don't think it can get any worse.

My mission was a success, so I don't think I should push my luck any further. As we get into the car, I start up and accelerate to maintain an appropriate speed.

-Have you regained your courage? -Can asks me with a twist.

-We only have one spare tire.

70

-Yes. Luckily I can book a few rooms at the hotel where Arzu is staying.

-Book? Aren't we coming back tonight?

-After we spend the morning on the road

I agree. I haven't fully appreciated the consequences of my plan. I'm afraid to call Mom later because I'm sure she's going to create a gruesome story in her head, imagining all the trouble I might have gotten myself into.

-Do you think Arzu will accept the role? -I ask. I hope my plan was worth it.

-I don't know. That's why I want to talk to her personally. For some reason, she turned down our initial offer and is not responding to Deren's calls. I'm afraid she may have received another offer from the company which the spy who leaks our projects works for.

-Do you know anything about the spy?

-Yes. Our leaks have benefited a company run by a former employee of ours-, Can explained to me as he sent a message on his cell phone. -My father fired her because of internal problems and we believe she wants to sink our company out of revenge.

Ayhan already warned me not to meddle in the espionage conflicts of big companies. My head will explode trying to find a connection between this and what Mr. Emre confessed to me.

-It is likely that this woman tried to hire Arzu. We'll find out when we meet with her.

My stomach rumbles. Thanks to my maneuvering, we're still in the middle of the highway at lunchtime. Only a nice plate of grilled meat would clear my mind after discovering the other conspiracy involving Can Divit.

CHAPTER IX

Amasra is one of my favorite coastal towns. I once came here on a trip with my family and even wrote a poem on the beach. Although today I don't have much time to enjoy it, as Can is like a caged tiger. In the hotel where Arzu is staying he has managed to get two rooms, although I sense that it has not been easy.

He asked for the actress. Luckily, the receptionist told us that she is leaving this afternoon. I feel like dancing, although the discussion with Mom has left me a little dazed. I've made up a meeting of the whole team so she doesn't get any funny ideas about Mr. Divit.

Mr. Can is going to his room. He'll take a shower, so I'll take his clothes to the laundry to make them presentable. While I'm talking to the front desk to have an employee brought to our room, Arzu Tas appears behind me. I am aware of her presence because a circle of admirers forms around her. In person her face is not as attractive as on TV.

-Miss Tas! -the receptionist calls to her. -Mr. Can Divit has taken an interest in you. He is staying at the hotel.

-Can Divit? -exclaims Arzu. Sometimes I forget that Can is also famous. -Please tell him I can meet him anytime.

-You can talk to his assistant-, the gossipy man lets go, pointing at me. -It's that young lady over there.

I smile as if I'd love to talk to the actress of the moment.

-Good afternoon, Miss Tas.

-Good afternoon-, she speaks to me as if I'm an insignificant fool. -You can tell Mr. Divit that I'd be delighted to meet him this afternoon.

I'll be in the hotel bar.

-I'll leave him your message.

She bids me farewell with a lazy, haughty wave of the hand, though to her it will be the height of politeness. I must keep her from meeting Can. This lizard will accept any favor or errand Can asks of her as long as she dupes him. I look at my cell phone. There is a missed call from Mr. Emre. I will inform him of the progress when we leave here.

Can returns to reception. He speaks to the receptionist to ask him to take care of the car.

-Mr. Can-, I whisper to him so the gossip doesn't give me away. -Miss Arzu left this morning.

-Don't worry, Mr. Divit. Miss Tas is going to postpone her reservation until she talks to you.

That man must have the ear of a bat. He'll love to hear all the gossip. At least he doesn't give me away, although when my boss turns around, he threatens me with a smirk. What does he want? Toss in some propine? The rich guy is my boss, not me.

-Perfect.

Can asks me to accompany him to his room.

-I want you to take my clothes to the dry cleaners. Then find Miss Arzu and ask her if she wants to meet me at the ferry the hotel is organizing.

Maybe this will fix my screw-up. Without wasting time, I go to the dry cleaner's and emphasize that I want my boss's clothes thoroughly cleaned.

-We'll have it ready in half an hour-, the manager assures me.

-No need to rush-, I assure him with my best innocent smile. -I'll pick it up in the afternoon.

Thanks to my ingenuity, Can won't be able to leave his room unless

74

he wants to make the staff's eyes happy. Then, to keep him from getting suspicious, I look for Miss Arzu. The actress is at the spa. First she has a sauna session and then a massage session. Patiently, I wait until I can join her in the massage session and, smiling wickedly at the sight of a room exclusive to spa employees, I tiptoe into it and change, becoming just another employee.

With a mask, no one will recognize me.

-Miss Tas-, I say, raising my voice to a higher pitch just in case. -Mr. Divit has left a message for you. He would like to take a bike ride with you in the bush.

Arzu squeals like a schoolgirl and her assistant mimics her. They awaken in me a feeling of revulsion for which I am grateful that I have put on my mask.

-Tell Mr. Divit I'll be waiting for him at six o'clock in the campers' square.

I nod and walk away, though I can hear them gossiping behind me.

-Arzu, it's a full-fledged invitation. Can Divit is a nature lover. I'm sure he's arranged a romantic getaway.

-Oh, sir, we're going to be the fashionable couple! -exclaims the diva.

-Hey, take it easy, you two!-, I snapped, startling everyone.

Arzu and his little lapdog glare at me. Damn, why does my strength go out of my mouth? Sometimes, I think I look too much like mom.

-I'm sorry. Mr. Can insisted it was a business meeting.

Before I make another blunder, I rush out of the spa and into the staff room, where I change back into Mr. Can's clumsy assistant.

I head for his room. In the meantime, I look at my cell phone. Mr. Emre has called me. He must be worried about the Arzu affair, so I try to get in touch with him, a difficult task, since in this five-star hotel coverage is a luxury service to which most of us mortals are not entitled.

-Mr. Emre?-, I greet him when I manage to call him. I try to ignore the whispers of the employees. It's enough for me to keep my balance on a sofa, begging for a little line of coverage.

-Sanem?-, I can barely hear his voice. -How was the trip?

-Terrible, although it went well. We arrived late at the hotel and your brother and Miss Arzu didn't manage to meet.

-Perfect. You must prevent them from talking at any cost.

-I'm on it, Mr. Emre. I'm arranging the meeting and I'm keeping them as far away from each other as I can.

-Thank you very much, Sanem. You prove to me every day that you can be trusted.

My chest swells with pride, but then I feel a bitter aftertaste, thinking of Mr. Can.

-I will not fail you. I promise you.

I shake off my regrets by reminding myself that Mr. Can is the one who plans to destroy his family's company for selfish reasons. Arriving at Mr. Can's room, I wait for him to show up to finish off the second part of my plan. There is no sign of my boss, so I pace around. I even fantasize about lying on his bed, since it's huge and I'm sure he sleeps there like in heaven.

-Sanem, where were you?

I turn around and almost die of a heart attack. Can is behind me, covered by a towel knotted around his waist. His chest is a miracle of anatomy. Every muscle looks like it's been chiseled, and on one of his pecs, my boss has a tattoo of a majestic albatross.

I open my mouth. Oh, my God. I must not drool, although my eyes stop and marvel at the drawing.

-It's an albatross. It's impossible...

-Yes, I had it done many years ago. Sanem?

It is impossible. It is a cruel game of destiny, which insists on associating my albatross with Can. But you mustn't lose your head. My boss interviewed me by quoting Baudelaire's albatross poem, so it's bound to be one of his favorite texts.

-Sanem? Are you listening to me?

-Of course, of course, sir.

-Where are my clothes?

Where they belong. Off your sculpted body.

-Sanem...

I shake my head. If Can doesn't think I'm stupid now, it's a miracle.

-It's at the dry cleaners. I'm told I'll have to pick her up in the afternoon, around six.

-That late? Then we won't be able to go down for lunch.

I don't mind. My hunger is being satiated by the divine gift of sight.

-I'll speak to room service if you don't mind, Mr. Can.

-Did you find Miss Arzu?-, he asks, trying to make eye contact with me. My goodness, dissimulation was not one of my virtues.

-No, I'm sorry. She's at the hotel spa. Sauna and massage session. I asked one of the masseuses to relay her message, as it was not right to interrupt Ms. Arzu at such a time.

-Perfect, Sanem-, he complimented me with a smile when I stopped staring at his prodigious musculature.

-I'm going to ask for your food to be brought to you. Although perhaps it's better if I bring it to you-, I add after speaking to my boss in a whisper. We don't want them to see your body so perf... To see you in this situation. It will be very uncomfortable for you.

-I appreciate you caring so much about me-,he says. His usual retinue causes his magic to disappear. However, when I go to my room, I will clear my head with a cold shower.

I leave that room of temptation. As my stomach rumbles, I rush to order food for two, although obviously we will each eat in our respective rooms. I don't want to tempt fate and I can't afford to take my clothes to the dry cleaners for staining while I'm distracted by Can's tanned skin.

For now, my plan is working perfectly. When I want to, I am a brilliant criminal mind. I have nothing to envy the corporate mole, although I act from noble motives.

After being handed two trays of appetizing food, I ask him to leave one in my room and take the other to Can's room. My boss is reading a novel in an armchair. He must have found it on the bedside table. It seems to me that luxury hotels offer this kind of entertainment to their guests.

Sitting there, Can resembles one of the tragic characters of antiquity. His appearance is beautiful, there is no other word for it. His every feature is a work of perfection, and yet his mind is profound. His hobbies do not correspond to those of a muscleman who only knows how to spend his time in a gym. Can is one of those rare examples where body and mind are perfect.

-Thank you very much, Sanem-, he greets me. The smell of the food must have caught his attention and I hope he was paying attention to the tray instead of my self-absorbed face.

-I let you eat alone-, I say goodbye. I have yet to bow to that fairytale prince.

We say goodbye and I return to my maid's quarters. Although the luxurious furniture and the bed try to deceive me, I know I am not a princess. I sleep here thanks to Mr. Can, because I work for him. I am a first-class maid. That's all.

At least I know what my position is and I don't let my two bosses down. Both Emre and Can thank me for every detail I carry out without screwing up, even if my wild poet lives deluded in a fantasy in which I fulfill his every wish.

I pounce on my plate like a wild beast. With each bite as I devour a zero-calorie salad and a chicken fillet that satisfies the rich snobby snobs who visit this hotel, I remind myself that I am here on a mission.

To stop Can from talking to Arzu Tas.

CHAPTER X

Can comes out of his room. Once again he is a bold explorer ready to take on the world. Every step he takes is a bump that shakes the carpet that runs down the hallway. I guess spending a good part of the afternoon locked half-naked in his room is not in good taste.

I glance at my wristwatch mischievously. It's half past six in the evening. If we go to the rich ferry, we'll meet a lot of actresses, but none of them would be Arzu Tas.

-Let's go, Sanem. It's very late. We mustn't keep Miss Arzu waiting.

Let her wait. I'm sure it will do her good to lower her inflated ego a little. Let's go out. The campers' square where I told Arzu to wait is in the opposite direction from the ferry. We head that way. It's still early, although it's starting to get dark. The sky is tinged with a yellowish hue and reflects its light on the sea. It is a very romantic landscape and, fortunately, Can and Arzu cannot share it.

It's a pity.

Can asks for Miss Arzu. On that ferry, people with money spend their afternoons snacking and enjoying the latest music. This is a floating disco. An extravagant luxury for my taste, although there are so many people blabbing around here that Can is not surprised not to find Arzu Tas.

The ferry pulls away from the harbor. It's going for a ride along the coast. Can sighs, leaning over the side. The clouds take on a beautiful orange hue. I'm inspired by the lines of a poem, though there's no one to share them with but Can.

-This woman is very elusive. I'd say she loves to be chased.

I laugh. I like that he talks about Arzu that way. It sets him apart from the rest of the people drooling after her for her fame.

-I'd say she's not here-, I opine, knowing I'm absolutely right. No one has seen her and an actress of her stature would attract all the attention.

-True-, he says with a deep sigh. He looks tired and disappointed. I feel a mysterious dagger stab into my heart. -Would you like to spend the afternoon with me? I don't want to talk to anyone else today about Arzu Tas.

I am happy, as only those who see their deepest longings fulfilled can be. These feelings confuse me, but I just want to live them. There will be time to think about work and conspiracies when we return to land.

-I have traveled a lot, but I have rarely been to Amasra, and when I have come here, it has always been on business. It has been impossible for me to enjoy this landscape-, he confesses.

-I used to come here with my family on vacation, although we used to do it more often-, I tell him, watching the sunset with him. -My sister and I would run along the beach collecting shells and I would make up a thousand stories about the couples we saw kissing in the harbor until I discovered the story about the forgotten maiden.

-What story is that?

It's a legend told to me by a little old lady at a street stall. Maybe it's a tale she made up, but the story exudes magic and has been with me ever since I was a child. It's strange to tell it to my boss. I watch him. He is watching me, as if what he is about to hear is the most wonderful thing in the world.

-A long time ago-, I begin, -a young couple swore eternal love to each other. On that cliff over there.

I point to the place that the little old lady discovered for me so long ago. Can doesn't miss any detail of my words and I close my eyes. I breathe in the scent of the sea and her cologne.

-But they had to part-, I say, lost in my memories. -He had to go on a voyage. It was not known if his ship would return, but he promised his beloved that nothing could separate them, and she promised that she would wait for him in the same place where they sealed their love.

-Did he return as the albatross? -the man standing next to me, the one with the two faces, the wonderful prince and the dark king, asks me, whispering.

-Never. Year after year, the woman waited for her beloved. He never returned and she became known as the forgotten maiden. However, at her death she asked that her ashes be thrown down the cliff because the wind would bring back the memory of her beloved.

Can watches the cliff without blinking. I would like to know his thoughts.

-It's a sad story. He might have forgotten it.

-We can't know how real his love was. Love is based on trust. If his feelings were pure and sincere, we can't judge her for waiting indefinitely.

-I think you're right. Have you waited for someone?

I deny sadly. I know love by hearsay except for one night when a stranger kissed me. My albatross. I should have answered him when he asked my name. Fear prevented me from unveiling the mystery of that kiss and now my only hope is to meet him again, but I am not like the forgotten maiden. My love lies in a one-way feeling, it is based on an illusion. I am like Ayhan's brother, Osman. Since he was a kid, the poor guy has been in love with Leyla although for my sister he has always been a friend, but he remains faithful in his feelings. He is an attractive man who arouses passions among women. However, his heart belongs only to Leyla.

-And you? -I ask him.

-Are you back to informality again?

I don't answer. I want him to.

-I am the lover who travels. I have made him wait too long.

I regret my curiosity, for I don't know what he meant. Is there a woman waiting for him in a port? Is he in love or is he just a man whose love only lasts for a season?

We remain in silence contemplating the landscape until the moon appears to accompany us. We are both immersed in our musings and I am only glad that I succeeded in keeping Can away from Arzu Tas.

Upon returning to the hotel, my boss doesn't ask about the actress, although he leaves a message to tell her he wants to talk to her in the morning.

-Do you want to have dinner at the port?

That invitation makes me happy, especially since it will keep Can distracted from work. The stars light up the sea and spread across the sky like little fireflies that have lost their way because they wanted to touch the moon. We go to a restaurant in the harbor where we hear the murmur of the waves. I didn't remember Amasra like that as a child.

-The grilled fish is delicious-, Can recommends.

We order two plates and I'm about to lick my fingers. Can and I talk about our favorite singers, as there is background music. Then he asks me to tell him about my childhood reading.

-Why?

-There's no better way to get to know a person.

And why does he want to know me? It's a mystery that distresses me, though it also ignites a small spark of excitement in my chest. I answer Can, I tell him about the stories with which my father used to say good night to me, later I confess the poems that made me fall in love as a teenager and the first novel that encouraged me to become a writer.

-And what did you read as a child?-, I am interested to remove the mask of that man who tries to captivate me.

-There were many books in my family's house. My mother was fascinated by reading and always read fables or poems to Emre and me.

His smile is permeated with sadness. I want to caress him and tell him I'm sorry for reminding him of his mother. The pain of his past has not gone unnoticed by me. His eyes squealed that his mother is a cherished memory.

-She also loved to travel and spoke many languages. She would tell me legends of the countries she visited and encourage me to learn other languages by giving me books I couldn't understand. I confess that I have been luckier than other children. Without my mother, I would not be the way I am now.

This is not a working dinner. I fiddle with the lettuce accompanying my fish fillet. I know that going back to Amasra will be different because of this trip.

-When are we going back to Istanbul?

-When Arzu Tas deigns to talk to me. I hope we will return home tomorrow. I am sorry to cause you so much inconvenience. We will compensate you for the overtime.

In the end my talk with Can really is a short break from work. I have to remind myself that he hasn't invited me to spend a weekend in this tourist town, but is looking for the woman who will star in his movie.

-The barbecue here is also unforgettable-, Can tells me. I can hear his voice, hanging on my half-empty plate. -If we're still here tomorrow, I'd like to treat you to one. There's nothing better than enjoying the moment.

I nod, lifting my head, smiling at him.

-I'd love to.

The next morning, as I wake up, I think about Can's invitation to have dinner with him tonight. If I can keep him from talking to Arzu Tas, I'm sure I can share the roast he recommended.

I groom myself diligently. I will be my boss's shadow. Emre trusts me. I call Can's room very early. I am afraid to wake him up. However, this man knows no fatigue. He invites me in. He is already dressed and is still reading the hotel novelette.

-Good morning, Sanem. You're an early riser.

What time did he wake up? I imagine him contemplating the sunrise, reading and remembering his mother and the stories she told him.

-I don't like to sleep too much.

-That's where we're alike. You can only enjoy the surprises of every-day life when you're awake.

I nod. What surprise will this trip have in store for me today?

-If you don't mind, I'd like you to call the front desk and ask for Arzu.

He points to the phone in the room, so he'll hear my conversation. I'm afraid that on this occasion I will be forced to sharpen my wits to the maximum.

-Good morning, I am Mr. Divit's assistant-, I introduce myself to the receptionist. -We would like to know if we could meet Miss Arzu Tas today, or if she has left a message for him.

-Good morning, Miss-, the clerk replies politely. I sweat. I can't think how to separate two people who want to see each other at any cost, especially when one of them is pursuing dishonest ends. -Miss Tas has asked us to inform you that they are waiting for you in the dining room. They are having breakfast and will not leave until they see Mr. Divit.

I swallow. This is a dead end.

-Thank you very much.

I hang up. Can doesn't take his eyes off me. The actress is Arzu, not me, so I'll have to be honest.

-Miss Arzu is waiting for you in the dining room. They told me at the front desk that she won't leave until she talks to you.

-Hallelujah! -Can exclaims, clearly satisfied. -Let's take the opportunity to have breakfast with her.

I nod, even though I want to dunk my head in the bathtub. With my bad luck, I'm sure Arzu recognizes me as the spa employee and will tell Can about my shenanigans. My only hope is that she's so enraptured with my boss that she won't pay any attention to me.

We headed for the dining room. As promised, Arzu is met by his assistant, who signals that we are approaching. Using his natural elegance, Can introduces himself and takes a seat with them. I imitate him. If I stand, I'm sure I'll attract more attention.

-I'm glad to finally be able to talk to you, Miss Tas.

-Oh, please, Can. Don't be so formal, we've already met-, she says with a laugh that's faker than a Monopoly ticket.

-Really?-, says Can, surprised. -I'm ashamed of my bad memory.

-Yes, at the Christmas party your father organized last year. We spoke very little, but you were very affectionate with me.

I'll bet their conversation was a hello and goodbye.

-Oh, right-, It's obvious that I've hit the nail on the head by Can's tone of voice, although as he's desperate to sign her up for the project, he plays along. -Well, it's good to see you again, Arzu. I promise you that this I will give you my undivided attention.

My stomach churns. Arzu's assistant smiles at me like a diabolical porcelain doll and beckons me with her eyes to sit further away from the couple, although I won't move unless my boss explicitly orders me to.

-That's a pleasure to hear, Can. It's a shame that the hotel employees had us pacing back and forth. I'm going to file a complaint.

I hope that witch bites her tongue and poisons herself, even though I was responsible for making the employees suspicious.

-That won't be necessary, Arzu. Let's enjoy the present. I'm sure that by talking we will soon forget yesterday's unpleasant incident.

At least neither of the two harpies recognizes me, although the reason for that is that one of them is amusing herself by devouring Can with her eyes.

-Perfect. I suppose you'll want to have a little more private conversation.

For the first time, that trashy actress notices me.

-I think it might be best if you're more comfortable. Sanem, you can take the morning off. I'll see you at lunchtime.

-Of course, Mr. Divit-, I say, getting up. -Miss Tas, it was a pleasure to meet you.

I would have preferred to butter your silky soft hair. Now that would have been a treat. I say goodbye to Can. Arzu's assistant accompanies me as if we were soul friends. However, once we are far enough away from the two supermodels, she separates from me as if I were going to give her the plague. Deep down, I'm grateful for it because then she won't get in the way of my plans.

During the morning I spy on my boss, who is laughing with Arzu. I can't hear their conversation. After a while, the two leave the cafeteria. I follow them slyly. Absorbed, neither of them pays any attention to me. They head for their room. I tiptoe around, hiding behind the plants in the hallway, until I discover that they enter Can's room. Arzu makes no secret of her excitement. I don't know what madness has formed in her overflowing imagination. She must think Can is going to propose to her.

I rush into my room. As I doubt that they are going to talk in bed, I go out to the terrace, from where I will be able to listen to Can and

Arzu's conversation if they have gone out like me. Sure enough, I hear the cackling of the actress.

-Can, you were right!-, says Arzu. -My social networks are on fire!

I take out my cell phone. If she's announced her signing with the Divit studio, I won't be able to talk to Mr. Emre with my head held high. I go on Arzu's Instagram and look at her latest photo, that of a plump girl who would be about sixteen years old. I read the attached text. That way I find out what it's all about.

"Sometimes it's complicated to show that the only thing that matters is the inside. This is me at seventeen and I was the same girl. There is no difference between this past and the present in which I have to thank you for your support. My biggest wish is to work hard so that what shines the most about me is my talent.

I can't believe people believe such a load of nonsense. With the little I had seen of Arzu Tas, the only thing that had dazzled me was her falsehood and her airs of repellent rich girl. Truly, the world loses its brains with actresses.

-So, can I count on you to be the star of my next movie? You don't have to be afraid of Aylin anymore-, says Can.

I run like hell. We have to separate them. I might as well set the hotel on fire. Thanks to that crazy thought, I come up with a great idea.

I look for a fire alarm. It doesn't take me long to find one, so I act like in the movies. I break the glass with a shoe, I didn't need to cut my hand either, and set off the alarm.

The guests immediately come out of their rooms and I start screaming like a hysterical woman.

-Fire! There's a fire! We have to get out of here!

I run in circles and chaos ensues. Arzu and Can come out of their room and the actress runs like a mad cow. She even pushes some hotel employees who have come to investigate the cause of the commotion.

Can stops next to me. He is the only one who remains calm. Crossing his arms, he looks at me mockingly.

-Sanem, what are you doing?

-The fire alarm has sounded. We have to get out of here.

Can smiles and urges me to leave, putting his hand on my back. I flinch at his touch. We walk away from the mess I've made with the fire alarm, so I breathe calmly, letting my boss lead me on.

-I think I've managed to convince Miss Arzu-, Can confides. My goodness. Nothing I've done has been worth it. -Unfortunately, she loves to keep things interesting, so I'll have to have dinner with her. I'm sorry, Sanem.

I shuffle my feet. Discouragement stiffens my muscles. I don't feel like walking. I can't bring myself to talk to Mr. Emre and confess to him that I have failed.

At the reception, we meet Arzu Tas. A female employee is reassuring her. It's not as if she had really set the hotel on fire, although I'm tempted if I find out which room is hers.

Can stays with her. Luckily, we don't put up with her for long, for when she regains her composure, she says goodbye, saying she must get ready for dinner. I look at my watch. Yes, it's time for lunch. Everything about this woman makes no sense.

-Are you all right, Sanem?-, Can asks me.

-Yes. It's been an exhausting two days. Maybe I could use some sleep.

-Yes, I think you're right.

He walks me to my room. I lie down on the bed. I can't get to sleep, thinking about Mr. Emre, although the greatest discomfort comes from imagining Can and Arzu having dinner. Although there is nothing else that depends on me.

I don't eat. In the afternoon Emre calls me. I tell him what has happened. My boss insists that I have done my best. My voice will have to clearly convey my state of mind. So Emre does not tell me what I deserve to hear.

The afternoon passes uneventfully and I see the Amasra sunset again, although this time I watch it locked in my room. In the evening, I get hungry and my steps take me back to the harbor restaurant. I sit alone and, with a bittersweet feeling, I order the dish recommended by Can. The menu includes salad and a bowl of baked potatoes.

I eat slowly, my eyes fixed on my plate, and am brought out of my reverie by the creak of a chair dragging. I look up and am surprised to find Can sitting with me and stealing a baked potato with a mischievous grin.

-It's hard to dine with an actress-, he says as if it's the most obvious thing in the world. -Most of them are on horrible diets and I hate eating alone. Don't you?

I nod, unable to articulate a single word. My eyes sting. Can calls a waiter over and orders the same dish as me.

-I prefer to dine with you. The conversations are more interesting too.

This is not a working dinner. This is our night. Can may not be my albatross, but I wouldn't trade him for anyone now. The next day I'd remember he's a scoundrel intent on sinking the family business; now he's just the man I can talk to about books or faraway places. The one who reveals aspects of the world I would never have imagined.

-Anyone would say you're like one of those movie stars-, I reply. This time, I'm the one who makes fun of the other.

-Yeah, but you know that's not true-, he replies, and it's impossible to deny it.

Can is not like anyone I've ever met before.

CHAPTER XI

I get in the car with Can. Tonight we say goodbye to Asmara. The moon is shining in the sky. It is nine o'clock. I put on my seat belt yawning and Can turns on the radio and tunes in to a classical music station. Slowly, I drift off to sleep to the company of violins and a piano in the background. I am not an expert in classical music. I ignore the name of the composer and, of course, the name of the piece.

I nod in my seat. Can drives absolutely calmly. He has told me that he doesn't mind driving without a license, that if he gets caught by the police, he will pay the fine. There is no one who understands this man.

I close my eyes. I dream of an albatross flying over the sea at sunset. It approaches land, not my beloved Galapagos, but the coast of Asmara. It perches on the cliff of the forgotten maiden and spreads its wings. His wingspan is majestic. He is the lord of the birds. In the distance, a shimmering bird approaches him. A golden light bathes its wings. I do not recognize the creature. However, my heart trembles with tenderness and pride. There is something about this bird that feels familiar and awakens a sense of warmth in me.

-Sanem-, Can calls me gently. The warmth spreads from my chest to my whole body. -Sanem, wake up. I've spoken to your mother.

I jump up and down. The worst of my nightmares has come true. I no longer think of the birds that are going to meet at the forgotten maiden's cliff.

-What?!

-Sanem, calm down. It was nothing serious. Your phone kept ringing and, since it's late and you didn't wake up, I answered it so as not to scare your mother. I'm sorry. I already apologized to your mother for bringing you here so late.

Can tries to apologize, but his damn smile gives him away. I'm going to bite my nails off in one bite out of sheer nervousness. I don't get any better when I recognize the streets Can is driving down. We're in my neighborhood.

Oh, my God. I want to die. At least this time, Can isn't driving his high-end SUV or a luxury sports car like his brother. However, if there is one characteristic that applies to our female neighbors, it's a passion for gossip. If any of them see Can, I'll have to put up with weeks of gossip.

-You can leave me here, Can. I'll walk.

-Don't be like that, Sanem. Besides, I want to say hello to your mother.

No. If my boss and my mother get together it will be an omen that the end of the world is near.

I notice with horror that in my street the neighbors are peeping out of the front door and the others are gossiping from the balcony. In front of my house, my mother chats with her friend Melahat. Somebody please kill me.

Can pulls up next to my mother. He rolls down the window and seduces her with a charming smile. Okay, I've thought better of what I want. I wish someone would fire my boss.

-Good morning, Mrs. Aydin. Sorry for the delay. Sanem just woke up.

My face is burning. I wish I had a paper bag to hide my face with.

-No need to apologize, Mr. Can. And call me Mevkibe, please.

Melahat looks at Can as if he were an endangered species, or rather a hallucination. It seems like the whole neighborhood is congregating around us. It's not as if we had arrived in a Ferrari.

With the commotion, my father also comes out to greet us and the scoundrel Can gets out of the car to take a bath with the masses.

-Good morning, Mr. Can. I'm Nihat, Sanem's father-, he shakes hands with him. -Would you like to join us for tea?

-I'd love to, Nihat. I am a great lover of tea.

And of inordinate attention. I jump into the street and push my way home. Out of the corner of my eye I catch a glimpse of Ayhan, drooling with Can. I guess she never thought she'd meet him in person. The worst thing is not that, though, but Misifu is approaching, fussing. I wish the world would end. The best thing that could happen is for a meteor to fall and destroy Istanbul.

-Sanem! Light of my life! What are you doing with that man?-, I hear him whimper.

Can turns to me.

-Is he your fiancé?-, he asks, looking at my ring.

-Him?! Never!

With any luck, Misifu will have heard and if I'm glad everyone is noticing Can, it gives me time to hide Mr. Emre's ring before someone sees it and adds to the rumors.

Can lets out a laugh and allows my mother to lead him inside the house.

-No, Mom! Mr. Can will be tired. Tomorrow is late and we have to go to the office. We'd better go to bed. All of us!

There are some gossipy people who take the hint and hide in their burrow. Can is still lingering around, letting himself be loved by Melahat and my mother.

-If you like, I can offer you one of my pasties for the road-, says Melahat.

-I can make him some croquettes that we had for dinner-, Mom jumps in.

-My wife makes the best croquettes in Istanbul-, my father intervenes. Only Leyla is left to join the party. Luckily, my sister is discreet. The only one with brains in the family, and she's probably inside the house, waiting to hear all about it.

-I won't say no to croquettes and *empanadillas*. I'm starving and I love home cooking.

I pull my boss. I take him to the car. In other circumstances, I would have been afraid he would fire me. Now all I care about is getting this duplicitous beau away from my family before he's adopted. However, Melahat and Mom were aware of our arrival and are quick to give him a lunch box each with croquettes and pasties. I'm sure they must have competed to see who could put the most food in their respective lunchboxes.

-They are very kind-, Can says goodbye, finally getting into the car. -I hope to see you another day for some tea.

-Come by anytime-, Dad offers.

-Thank you so much for taking care of Sanem-, Mom says. A little more and she kisses his hands and offers me as his wife.

Can smiles at me with his usual superior gesture, starts up and drives off. I sigh in relief.

-Sanem, who is that?-, Misifú whines at my back. He's the only one of the neighbors, next to Ayhan, who hasn't left.

-It's my boss, Muzaffer-, I tell him, about to jump down his throat, and not as he would wish.

-Why did you tell him I wasn't your fiancé? Your parents are going to give me your hand. We are fated for each other.

My mother approaches. At first her aim would be to accost me with questions about Can. But with Misifu around, she knows I'm not in the mood. At least my childhood friend's heavy-handedness has come in handy tonight.

-Muzaffer, the decision to marry is up to Sanem-, Mom interjects. I hope she always remembers that we are now living in the 21st century.

-But what about the dinner between our two families? I can't get to sleep because I'm so anxious to seal our love at last.

I am grateful that Can has left. If he hadn't, he would have missed the popcorn and with his stupid grin he would have unhinged me to the point that I would have been imprisoned for murder. Of whom? I don't know. Maybe I would be tried for multiple murder.

Dad takes it upon himself to mediate between Misifu and Mom. I wish him luck because Muza's mommy is coming too, so she and my mother will be pulling each other's hair out in no time. At home, Leyla is sitting on the couch. Her expression is serious. She is probably itching to lecture me about my boss, although she has no reason to. In the eyes of the gallery, I have only followed the instructions of my superiors. That they were unaware that my time does not belong to them alone is not my problem.

-Is there any news about the analysis of your laptop?-, I was interested like a good little sister.

-No. I'm still on vacation-, Leyla replies, wishing she was my mother and could scold me to her heart's content.

-It's a pity.

Since I've already had dinner and I don't have a hole in my stomach like Can, I go up without tasting Mom's meatballs. Ayhan calls me on my cell phone. I sigh. I must get used to gossip from now on.

-Sanem, what happened?

-We had to travel to Asmara. The studio wanted to hire Arzu Tas as the star of their first movie and Mr. Can was supposed to meet her in person.

-And what were you doing there? Are you still meddling in the Divits' family affairs?

-No, I'm not-, I said. Well, I'll explain it better later. -I'm Mr. Can's personal assistant, so in meetings like this I have to go with him.

-If only I were you, my dear-, Ayhan purrs mischievously. I imagine what she fantasizes about.

-Well, I'd like to be in your shoes. I've had two crazy days. Arzu Tas is a repellent who only wants to seduce Mr. Can…

-Logical and normal.

-Yes, Ayhan, but she's a bad woman.

-Shouldn't you care? It's not like you're in love.

-What are you saying?!

-Okay, okay. You're upset from a professional perspective. You want the best for your boss.

I must be the most hated woman in all of Istanbul today. Ayhan keeps laughing at me, so I wish her good night and go to bed. The mattresses in my hotel room were top of the line. However, there is nothing more comfortable than your own bed and, without even undressing, I closed my eyes, ready to sleep.

Tomorrow it would be my turn to put up with mom.

-Sanem! -she shrieks at me.

I'm about to burst into tears. The day couldn't possibly end any worse.

-What's wrong, Mom?

My parents come into my room. I'm glad I didn't undress because they don't know the meaning of the word intimacy.

-That's what I want to know. Why didn't you tell me you were going on a trip? Why didn't you answer my call? If Mr. Can hadn't talked to me...

Now I have to put up with my mother talking about the goodness of my scoundrel of a boss.

-Mom, I'm Mr. Can's assistant until I get my first design. They ask me for everything. I don't even know what's waiting for me in the office tomorrow.

-Mevkibe, Sanem can barely stand up. Her boss has escorted her home, so there's nothing to be sorry about. We'll talk to her tomorrow.

My mother is reluctant to release her prey. I can still draw a little more blood.

-It's okay. Rest, sweetheart.

They leave and I stifle a scream into my pillow. Sleep, I just want to sleep for a few hours before I go to work in that messy office. Was I asking for too much?

The next morning, neither Mom nor Leyla say anything to me, although their eyes are much more sincere. They judge me. They think that at any moment I will make a mistake and screw up. It's not normal that in just a few days I'm my boss's shadow. I'm sure they think I'm being supervised so they can kick me to the curb at the first opportunity.

I go to the office like a soul in pain. I'd trade my soul for a shoulder massage. Last night's nap in the car stiffened my neck. Ceycey and Güliz pounce on me when they see me.

-Good morning, Sanem, how was the Asmara trip?-, Ceycey asks me.

-Hey, you! The new one!-, Deren calls out to me. You'd think with the days I've been away she could have learned my name. -There's a lot of work to do! No slacking off!

I put up with Arzu Tas yesterday. I clench my fist and Ceycey placates me by massaging my shoulders. He's an angel fresh from heaven.

In the morning, I return to my intern routine. The only joy will come at the end of the month with my paycheck when I get the money I've been promised for overtime.

During the break, Güliz shows me two fellow albatross candidates. At a glance, I rule them both out. For now, my albatross stays hidden. The only one I've come across is the tattoo on Can's chest. Not for a second do I consider telling Güliz or Ceycey about what happened at the hotel, the ferry or the restaurant. My conversations with Can are a little treasure I don't want to share with anyone, mostly because I feel a little guilty. Is my love for the albatross so pure if I'm turned off by the first attractive man who crosses my path?

I watch Can, strolling among the employees, greeting them as if he were one of them and not the boss. I know his true personality, the one hidden between the layers of goodness. No one can be that perfect.

At lunch, I get used again to sharing the table with people on my level. Ceycey, Güliz and I were born to, at best, laugh at the upper class. My story is not Cinderella. The only miracle that has happened to me is meeting my albatross. There is no reason to miss Can's conversation, his laughter, his voice beside me at sunset.

-Tomorrow we're going to record in a back room-, Deren informs us. -Ceycey, your duty is to see that tomorrow the catering is in perfect condition for the actors.

-So far there have been no complaints, Deren. Trust me.

Ceycey winks at Güliz and me and puffs out his chest like a turkey.

-I wouldn't gamble my job so quietly if I were you-, Deren scolds him. -Tomorrow Arzu Tas is coming. She's going to sign the contract and meet the studio, so everything must be perfect. You, the new one, will be Ceycey's assistant. I don't want you to be distracted for anything in the world.

I open my mouth. I want to let Deren know everything I think of her. However, there is one matter of high priority.

-My name is Sanem, not new one. I've been with this company for a few days now, you could have learned my name by now!

Güliz and Ceycey look pale. I myself don't believe what I've just done. Maybe I've been too emboldened by the confidence I've taken Can into my confidence. My dismissal is coming. Ceycey covers his face, terrified.

-What's going on here?-, Can asks. Oh sir, I'm sure you've been attracted to my screams.

-Excuse me, sir, the new girl...

-Her name is Sanem, Deren. We must respect our employees so that they respect us. Call her by her name.

Now it's the harpy who's stunned. I don't even dare to breathe.

-I understand, Mr. Can.

The man I loathe for infuriating me at times and conquering me with his sweetness at others times walks away. Deren leaves too, though she tenses her lips first. I bet my hand she's dying to see me off.

-I don't want any mistakes tomorrow.

Ceycey and I nod.

Without giving me time to catch my breath, Mr. Emre calls me into his office. He looks as elegant and dainty as ever, with his fine imported suit and handkerchief in his pocket. Talking to him relaxes me in spite of the tasks he has given me.

-Sanem, I asked Deren to put you and Ceycey in charge of the catering.

-Yes, sir. I have already spoken to her.

-Tomorrow Arzu Tas is coming and it's vitally important to make her stay as uncomfortable as possible-, Emre whispers to me. -The woman is a great actress, but it's Can's selfish desire to make the film his way and sell the company. You have to get her to back out of the project and I will defend you if she accuses you of anything. After all, Arzu is a maniac and it's easy for her to lose her temper.

I smile. I adore Mr. Emre and sometimes what he asks of me are the most rewarding tasks.

CHAPTER XII

I have never been on a shoot until now. Before, I only knew what I read in magazines or what was shown in documentaries. Being deluded, I discover today that there is no magical atmosphere behind the scenes. Ceycey and I run around catering to movie star whims, although to be honest, the only one who abuses the others is Arzu Tas, and I am her personal slave.

Curiously, Arzu, unlike Deren, calls me by my name constantly, although she pronounces it with disdain. For a reason unknown to me, she hates me. Although she always smiles at me, I sense a corrosive hatred. If it were up to her, I would end up at the bottom of the sea with chains on my feet.

-Did something happen between you two in Asmara? -Ceycey whispers to me after Arzu refuses a cup of coffee I brought her because, according to her, it was not at the right temperature, even though it came from the same coffee pot from which the whole cast drinks. -In the end, we're both going to get fired.

Ceycey is sweating like a chicken. This shoot must be more stressful than usual. I'm surprised Arzu Tas has so many fans. The only one she treats like a human being is Can. She spends the morning clinging to his arm, laughing at him, even though Can is also on the verge of a nervous breakdown. She laughs in a forced way. Arzu delays shooting because of her eccentricities and I've heard actors ranting about her. If I didn't run the risk of being kicked to the curb, I would have joined the huddle. I'm sure that if I asked for advice on how to get rid of Arzu, I would receive many proposals, each one more aggressive than the last.

-Sanem, forget about coffee. All I drink are detox shakes. Haven't you looked into my diet?

I'm thankful the knives are guarded by Ceycey.

-I'm sorry for my absent-mindedness, Ms. Arzu. I'll make you one right away.

I've heard about detox smoothies from Leyla, who is vegan. I don't know what's in them, though. I approach Ceycey and repeat to myself that I shouldn't ask her for a knife.

-Ceycey, how do I make a detox smoothie?

-A smoothie? What do you want a smoothie for? -My friend is barely breathing because of how fast he's talking. -We'd have to get a blender and there's no time.

-Ceycey, calm down. Take it easy. There's a blender over there-, I say, pointing to a corner of the table we've set up as a kitchen. I just want to know what to put in a detox smoothie.

-Oh, okay. I don't know what I'd do without you, Sanem.

Ceycey walks me to the fridge and tells me that the detoxes have antioxidant greens in them. I wrinkle my nose at the ingredients in one of those smoothies. It's normal for Arzu to be so bitter if that's what she feeds on. I'm surprised she hasn't turned into a rabbit.

I take lettuce, celery, cabbage and put it in the blender. The resulting color kills my appetite. Actually, I have a problem with my taste for meat. I should balance my diet, but I love to eat. It's one of my favorite activities and I don't like to suffer with it.

I go back to where Arzu is. They keep photographing her in front of the set that simulates the structure of a bridge. In the background, there is a mural of a coastal city, so I imagine they are now taking a few promotional images.

Mr. Emre and I exchange a glance. I can't think of what to do to get rid of Arzu. She reminds me of a cockroach: although she protests at everything, she is indestructible. It would survive a nuclear explosion.

-Sanem, the smoothie is for lunchtime-, she says with a loud sigh. -Really, my dear, you are so simple.

Deren, who is also watching the photo shoot, grits his teeth.

-There are flies in this studio. Haven't you fumigated it? I thought it was a high-class facility-, the bitch rants now.

-Arzu, it's impossible to get rid of all the insects-, Can interjects. -Ignore them. They won't bite you.

-But Can-, she replies in a falsely pitiful voice. -I'm sure Sanem knows how to solve the problem so that an actress of my stature is at ease.

I open my mouth, but I close it as I come to my senses. I've been about to tell that posh girl that there's only one reason why flies are swarming around her and that I can't work miracles. However, I nod and smile meekly.

-Of course, Miss Arzu. There is a foolproof method.

If I didn't have Mr. Emre's protection, I wouldn't dare commit such a folly. I go to the kitchen I share with Ceycey and ignore her pleas.

-What are you going to do, Sanem? My God, stop it!

I turn on the fire and put a pot on top. I throw in some brochures I have found around, open the fridge and throw in one of Arzu's favorite herbs. Soon a smoke rises from the pot.

-Sanem! We're going to get fired!

Later I will apologize to Ceycey if I haven't killed him. At this moment, I rush to the set where Arzu is the object of all eyes and walk my steaming pot.

-Sanem! -they all shout at me, including Deren. They have finally learned my name.

-It's a homemade method to scare off insects!-, I say. -It's a family secret!

Mom knows a lot of weird remedies, although if she heard me say that, she'd chain me to the bed and forbid me to leave the house again. My crazy idea works. The one who screams the loudest and gets the angriest is Arzu Tas. A sense of pleasure widens my smile.

-Sanem, that's enough-, Emre recommends. -We appreciate your remedy.

Since I don't want to see how much he is willing to put up with in order to get rid of Arzu, I return to the kitchen. The downside of my plan is that I now smell smoke and burnt vegetables.

I pour water into the pot, but it only causes more steam.

-Sanem, you're going to kill me-, Ceycey says to me, sweating profusely.

-It wasn't that bad. Do you see flies on the set?

Arzu whimpers on Can's chest. He's entertaining himself with her groping more than he should. The next, I put on a mask and shake it off with a bat.

-That's it, Arzu. It wasn't that bad-, Can consoles her, pulling her away from him, as it should be. -Let's just take a few more pictures and call it a day.

Arzu agrees. They ask her to suck on some candy and anyone would say that they have asked her to eat the concoction I have created in the pot because she kicks like a little girl.

-Can, I'm allergic to strawberries and there are strawberry-flavored candies here.

-Well, leave that one and eat the others while we take your picture.

Today Can has earned my respect for his patience. Anybody would have strangled that insufferable, trashy actress. It's obvious he desperately wants her for his movie.

Arzu obeys and eats the other candy with disgustingly suggestive poses, although Can and the others photograph her like true professionals without being fooled by her tricks. At the end, they end the call shift and we go to eat.

-Sanem, take Miss Arzu her milkshake-, Ceycey asks me.

I obey and go to give Miss Arzu her "healthy" drink.

-Are you here already? Have you put the smoothie in the fridge?

My hand shakes. I wonder if Mr. Emre's protection would help me if I smash the glass over his head.

-No, I'm sorry, Miss Arzu.

-I have to explain everything to you! You drink it at the right temperature! Now it will taste disgusting. Prepare another one!

I boil with rage. Maybe my intentions are obvious because Can takes the milkshake out of my hand.

-I don't think it's that big of a deal. I'll drink it myself.

I admire Can for taking that. Did he do it for me? His gesture remains unperturbed.

-It's a different taste. I prefer fruit smoothies, but it's not bad at all. Arzu, will you come with me to my office?

-Of course, Can-, she agrees. Her eyes sparkle. Sanem, take my smoothie to my office. I want it as fresh as possible.

I spew fire from my mouth. While the others pack up and leave for the office, I prepare a fresh smoothie. The temptation to spit on the celery is too powerful. Evil seduces me and I imagine a thousand and one ways to take revenge on Arzu. One of them is to make her swallow a boiling detox shake. However, I am inclined to be subtle. She's a whiner. I'm sure a couple of strawberries wouldn't hurt.

I throw the ingredients into the blender, including my two little strawberries, and the mucus green color is the same as before. Now all I have to do is laugh like the wicked witch in Snow White. But, hey, the joke has made my day a little brighter. I can't give this shake to Arzu. An allergic reaction is always dangerous, so I proceed to make her a proper smoothie.

I go back to the fridge. I repeat the operation from before, without adding the strawberries of death, and pour a nice glass of disgusting green drink while Ceycey collects everything around me. She keeps repeating that we're going to get fired. Poor guy, I'll make him a lime tea later.

Before I leave, I want to put the anti-Arzu shake in the fridge so it won't cause any damage, but I can't find it.

-Let's go back to the office, Sanem-, Güliz tells me. The cleaning service will pick this up.

-Hey, have you seen a glass of smoothie I left here?

-The detox? Yes, Ceycey took it to Arzu. Poor guy doesn't want you hanging out with her too much and I understand that. You scared me when you talked to her.

My legs are shaking. I almost fell and spilled the milkshake. I'm going to get fired for killing Arzu Tas.

I run as fast as I can. I must exchange glasses with Ceycey before misfortune strikes. I collide with several companions, though not a bit of milkshake falls out. I hear Deren yelling, but all I care about is Ceycey. He returns from a balcony where some employees are out for a smoke and where Can and Arzu are talking.

-What is it, Sanem?-, Ceycey asks. -I've already given Arzu the detox.

I push open the balcony door. Arzu is startled and chokes. The big gulper has already drunk half of it.

-What's wrong, Sanem?-, Can says. Nothing fazes him.

-I've brought another milkshake for Miss Arzu. The poor thing will be hungry, and with only one glass....

-Oh, that's very kind of you, Sanem-, for real no one can detect that any sympathy from that woman is feigned? -But I only have one glass at lunch. That's enough calories. You can go now. Thank you very much for the detox. It's delicious.

-Okay-, I mumble. Can doesn't take his eyes off me. He suspects me. If Arzu dies, I'm going to be the prime suspect.

-Go now, Sanem. Go on-, I'm being whipped by the damn diva. Maybe I'll get a prize for eliminating her.

No, let's not laugh at the situation. My neck is on the line.

I sit down in one of the armchairs we have to rest. It's lunchtime and I don't feel like having a bite to eat. My companions whisper happily about how the film is progressing. I don't dare to look at the balcony where Arzu is. I will scream when she starts convulsing and kicking.

-Oh, sir, she's going to pounce on Mr. Can-, Güliz says to me, -and by the look on his face I imagine she's going to be disappointed.

I jump on the couch. Like Güliz said, the harpy brings her face close to Can's. She only wants one thing. However, my boss steps back. He caresses her face. No. He gets scared. That's it. Arzu has minutes to live. She puts her hands to her cheeks. They start to swell. Oh, my God. If I can see it from here that means the reaction is a big one.

-Somebody call an ambulance! -Can yells back into the office.

Chaos ensues. No one notices me. I should run away. I'll start a new life in Bulgaria or Greece. I'll change my name or I'd better throw myself into the sea, so no one will find me.

Deren takes care of Arzu Tas, who hides in despair. Luckily for both of us, no one photographs her. My crime is still secret.

-Sanem, can I talk to you for a minute?

No one pays attention to us. If I hit him and knock him down, it will give me time to run. No way. Ridiculous. I'd never get Can down.

-What was in that milkshake?

-Vegetables-, I say, though I know the autopsy will give me away.

-Miss Arzu is not going to die-, Can whispers to me. -Although we know what she's like. At the hospital they will sort everything out. Maybe some strawberries fell into the blender. Did you clean it well?

-I don't know.

In his hand, Mr. Can holds Arzu's glass. He tastes it, he tastes like a taster.

-Delicious as Miss Arzu said. It has a very interesting sweet touch. I think I'm going to take a liking to detox drinks. May I finish that one too?

He points to the glass in my hands. This man is worse than a forensic scientist. My hands are shaking.

-I haven't eaten anything, Mr. Can. I'd like to drink it. Miss Arzu says they contain a lot of calories.

-I understand.

I drink the detox little by little. It tastes like lightning. How could it be good with so many vegetables? It's crucial that I don't look disgusted. We both laugh.

-I'll go to see Miss Arzu. Tell Ceycey to watch out for catering the next few days and take strawberries off the menu.

He knows I'm guilty. He waits until there's a dead body to report me to the authorities.

-I'll take care of everything, Sanem. Accidents happen every day.

I nod. I don't know how to take those words. Did he just threaten me? The only one trembling as much as I am is Ceycey.

-I'm going to get fired. I brought her the milkshake. I killed her. They're going to put me in jail-, he says over and over again like a parrot.

We both plop down on a couch and hold hands to share grief. The chaos in the office is total. However, I manage to spot Mr. Emre in the crowd.

He is preoccupied, but nods to me.

My goodness. I have become a hitwoman.

CHAPTER XIII

Arzu Tas' allergic crisis has even appeared in the tabloids. Mom explains it to me at dinner. Leyla and Dad comment on the care to be taken with the diet. I don't utter a word, but nod at key moments to show my assent.

It's been three days since my attempted murder, I mean accident. The police have not come to arrest me, so Arzu Tas has not reported me. Just in case Ceycey and I threw the blender and strawberries in the trash and promised not to talk about it again.

The only change that has happened in these three days is that Arzu will not be starring in the movie. We have already found a replacement and all the employees are happy with her, including Can. She is a very nice girl who always thanks us for everything.

I'm still Ceycey's assistant by Deren's express order, although Can still does small jobs for me from time to time. Luckily he is busy because we have two projects apart from the film. One is secret, although Güliz has told me that Can collaborates with companies owned by childhood friends of his. The other is a contest organized by a foreign company that would be good for us, as we would have an extra producer for the film. However, in order for us to be selected, the studio must pass an audit.

Mr. Emre has asked me that we should not pass the audit, because if Can gets such a sponsor, he will sell the studio on the wrong day.

So, I am sitting on a terrace with Ayhan scheming how to overturn the audit.

-I told you not to meddle in the Divit family feuds. Last time you almost killed Arzu Tas!

-I have no choice. Forty thousand lira, Ayhan. I don't know how to repay that debt.

-It's a good price for killing Arzu...

-It's not funny.

In the end, Ayhan decides to help me with my plan. If it goes well, the audit will definitely fail. Although my friend is reluctant to be my shadow hand. All this playing spies and sabotage is getting to me.

After finishing my secret meeting with Ayhan, I return to the office. Güliz and Ceycey are still lending me a hand with Operation Albatross, although none of our bearded colleagues meet all the requirements. I still haven't found the man who kissed me that night, which seems farther and farther away.

-Good morning, Ceycey-, I greet my friend, who is climbing the walls.

-Good morning to you, Sanem. Deren has put me in charge of supervising the cleaning of the office. Me! Overexploitation is the cause of bankruptcy, even for the best companies.

I calm him down. It would break my head to put up with Deren, though.

-They're going to fire me. I'm going to get fired-, Ceycey mutters.

I should repeat that, although Ayhan will be the one sabotaging the audit. Unless she's arrested and questioned, they won't be able to link her to me. In the morning I take care of copying reports and distributing them to the departments while I watch Ceycey duster even the plants.

Miss Deren approaches shortly before lunchtime.

-Ceycey, I need you to set up a break area.

-A break area?

-Yes, for the employees, but especially for the actors. We've found that's going to get a lot of points, so I want you to set it up before 5:00.

Ceycey is going to die today. He lays down on one of the couches. He could use someone to fan him, but the poor guy won't enjoy it until he finishes the rest area.

Before Deren gives me a meaningless task, I go to Ceycey.

-We can set up a sitting area next to the cafeteria. If we decorate it nicely, it will look very nice. Come on, I'll take care of everything.

I drag him to the cafeteria. My friend is a source of sighs. However, after moving the couches and placing them there, decorating it with flowers and printing some of my test designs and hanging them on the wall, the cafeteria is unrecognizable. It's not a trendy space, but it's homey. Ceycey settles into one of the armchairs. If he weren't terrified of Deren, he'd take a little nap right here.

And it's only half past four. I'm feeling unstoppable today.

-Come on, let's go show Miss Deren.

Although when we bring it to the rest area and show it to her, Deren is not as pleased as Ceycey.

-Whose idea was it to decorate it like this? -she asks with a frown.

-Sanem's-, Ceycey replies, not realizing the danger.

-Sanem, how could you come up with such stupidity? This is not worthy of the level of elegance of our studio. We can't show it to the auditors.

She hates me. From day one she has hated me. If Arzu disliked me, Deren is another level. She looks at me so fiercely that I don't feel like responding. I stammer. I can't bring myself to defend the decoration. After all, I've used practice designs to decorate the break area to be judged by a foreign company.

-Throw all this stuff away and when the auditors leave, put the chairs back.

Of course. It's the only logical solution.

Deren leaves. Now I'm the one who lies down on one of the chairs. Ceycey kneels down next to me and places a hand on my shoulder.

-Sanem, you know her. You mustn't make a big deal out of it...

-No, Ceycey. She's right. I'm a designer, but so far I haven't been asked to do anything. Just to carry folders, use the printer. I don't know why Mr. Can hired me in the first place. I guess they needed some bimbo to fill in as an intern.

Little tears fall on my lap. I take a breath because I don't want to burst into tears with Ceycey. I rub my face with my knuckles.

-Sanem, what you say is not true. You're wonderful and I'm glad you're my friend.

Friends. I want to hug Ceycey. However, Deren will tell him off if he stays with me. I spread my uselessness. I suffer from an incurable disease.

-Please go away. I feel like being alone.

He gives me my space and leaves. I remain with my idiotic designs and the ridiculous sitting area I set up to lend Ceycey a hand. What an idiotic thing to do, who could I possibly help with my talent? I remember when Can promised me he would commission designs for me soon. He's gone back on his word. I guess it was all just politeness.

I close my eyes. I take refuge in my albatross, in how he held me and protected me. With a kiss he made me forget about my uselessness. For a few brief, beautiful seconds I thought I was a princess, a woman who deserved to be loved.

Thank goodness I fled when he asked for my name. Thanks to that, I can treasure this memory.

-Sanem.

A warm voice calls out to me. It is a dream. My albatross comes to me. He strokes my face and massages my hair. Another tear slides down my cheek. He gently wipes it away.

-Sanem. Don't cry, please. This is beautiful.

I slowly open my eyes. Beside me stands Mr. Can, comforting me with a warm smile even though he must be attending to the auditors.

-Ceycey told me what happened. I'm so sorry, Sanem.

Hearing my name spoken by him softens my heart. His warmth heals the wounds inside me. For an instant, I almost shed the tears I need to wipe it all away.

More tenderly, he takes my hand and leads me out of the break area. In the office, my colleagues work tirelessly and Deren talks to the auditors. There is a lot of hustle and bustle in the office and I guess Ayhan has forgotten about our sabotage maneuver. Can bids me a fond farewell and meets with the auditors.

I take advantage of the fact that no one is paying attention to me and glance at my cell phone. I almost have a heart attack. There are seven missed calls and a message from my friend:

"It's already here."

Oh, Lord. Maybe I can still undo the sabotage maneuver. The audit is about to end. My shenanigans are now meaningless.

-A mouse! A mouse!-, Ceycey squeals.

There is a stampede. I back away from the mob. I jab the end of a desk into my kidneys. I imagine the mouse will be in the circle that has formed in front of a small filing cabinet.

-Calm down!-, Can asks, holding up his hands.

He is the only one brave enough to face the beast. He advances towards the mouse. The auditors tremble at the feat unfolding before their eyes. Kneeling down, with his bare hands, Can grabs the source of the chaos and lifts it up, raising it to the sky.

-It's a hamster! Please, keep your manners!

Oh, my goodness. Luckily, no one has discovered Ayhan, otherwise

I would have been in trouble and I wouldn't be able to look Mr. Can in the face again.

-What a shame!-, I hear one of the auditors say. —Never, in all my years of profession, have I ever witnessed anything like this.

Deren takes charge of the situation and dismisses the audit team. She repeats incessantly that this incident is not common in the company and it's of no importance, but her face says that she will skin the person responsible if she gets her hands on them.

-I'm going to be fired. I should have kept quiet-, stammers Ceycey next to me. I hug him, apologizing and thanking him for what happened in the cafeteria.

My friend relaxes as time passes and the routine returns to the office. It's not long before we leave and Mr. Emre calls me aside.

-Congratulations on the hamster, Sanem. Unorthodox, but certainly effective.

That doesn't cheer me up, it saddens me. He may be a bad guy at heart, but Mr. Can has been supportive and his words conveyed the sweetness I needed. In the absence of my albatross, he was there to shelter me with his wings.

-Thank you very much, Mr. Emre.

I bid him farewell and soon gather my things. Ceycey and Güliz accompany me to the exit. Mr. Can has announced that there will be an important meeting in the morning, so we must be on time.

I have a headache. Ceycey hugs me one last time before we say goodbye and assures me that the rest area was beautiful. Tomorrow it will be my turn to rearrange everything.

At home, I plan to eat dinner as quickly as possible and lie in bed. Maybe if I read a little my mind will clear and I will stop thinking about Mr. Can and the sweetness he always gives me.

My family is on the terrace where we usually eat in summer and receive visitors. My idea was to say goodbye and run away. However, when they hear me coming, they turn to me.

-Sanem!

Mom looks like she's got her rolling pin out. What have I done? Instead, Dad checks on her. He calls to me softly.

-Sanem, we found out you talked to the supplier.

Damn. Why does trouble pop up like mushrooms? Suddenly, they surround me and pepper me with questions about how I managed to raise the forty thousand lira. I pull my hair out. I don't feel like making up any stories, but the day has been so long that I don't want any more trouble.

-I asked for an advance at work, Mom-, I say in a fit of inspiration. -Dad has a heart condition and the supplier was threatening to sue us, so that's what I came up with. Mr. Emre gave me the advance and said he would take it out of my salary. In a year's time I will have paid off the debt.

-And what are you going to live on, Sanem? -my mother asks me. The anger with which she spoke to me before has disappeared.

-I live at home. I don't need the money.

-But you have to save, daughter. You have to think about the future-, my father intervenes.

Leyla comes to my side and puts an arm around my shoulders.

-Sanem, the family must stick together. You know, I've been reinstated at work. Mr. Emre interceded for me and assured me that it was impossible for me to be the spy for his company. I don't know if you talked to him in the end, but I don't want to ask. I will share half of my salary with you until we settle the debt.

My mother looks at us with moist eyes. Dad is dumbfounded.

-It can't be. I still remember when you were crawling around the house and now you're supporting us. How did you grow up so much?

-I'm so proud of you, my girls-, Mom says before hugging us.

Dad joins in and the four of us melt together like a sandwich. I can't believe the day ends like this, after so much suffering. I cry again. I cry because I'm a liar, I cheat everyone. Leyla is going to pay me half of her salary believing that I earn nothing when in fact it was Mr. Emre who saved our butcher shop.

I am useless, although this hug shows me that at least there is a place where I will always be loved and supported even though I am not with my albatross.

CHAPTER XIV

Because of Mr. Can's warning, I am up early and am the first to arrive at the office. Ceycey greets me with another hug. I love this man.

-I want to show you my admiration before Mr. Can fires me for yesterday.

-You're not going to get fired, man.

Although he might get the boot today at the meeting. The audit was a disaster thanks to me, so it's going to be unpredictable what will happen. After the Arzu thing, misfortunes keep happening. At least Mr. Emre won't be able to say that I don't measure up as his collaborator.

Can has gathered us around a table. Deren and Emre join him.

-The results of the audit will reach us in three days. We will probably be selected as one of the finalists despite what happened yesterday. Does anyone know how the hamster got into the office?

No one dares say anything. Ceycey shrinks so as not to draw attention to himself. I regret my plan. Hopefully there are no consequences for any of my coworkers.

-Well, that's not the most important thing. Yesterday we lost a lot of points in the audit for lacking a rest area. Why?

Deren steps forward. Now I'm the one who looks down and waits for the scolding.

-I gave it to Ceycey and asked Sanem for help. It was unqualified for this undertaking.

-Yesterday I went there and my opinion is different-, says Can. For the first time I hear him speak angrily. -We lost points in an important audit because you disregarded the work of an employee. If you think something is substandard, you should take it up with me or my brother, since we own the company.

-I... I'm sorry...-, Deren murmurs. I wouldn't want to be in her place bearing Can's wrath.

-You shouldn't apologize to me, but to Sanem. She is the one you have humiliated in front of other employees. One of the fundamental rules of this company is to maintain respect, and if we don't show respect to our subordinates, we can't demand it from them. I don't want anything like that to happen again with any other employee. Have I spoken clearly, Deren?

A murmur spreads around me. Many are pleased about Deren's reprimand and I hear words of approval for Can's speech. Right now he has just won the sympathy of the entire staff. Although I suppose I will arouse Deren's hatred again. I don't know how to take Can's defense. My boss disbands the meeting and we each return to our chores.

Ceycey breathes a sigh of relief that he won't be fired. I, on the other hand, bite my nails waiting for Deren to call me. She will vent her frustration on me. As my time comes, I open my design folder. I've been practicing sketches after learning the name of the film and my desk is full of albatross drawings. However, the only one who asks me to come to his office is Can.

-Good morning, Sanem.

My legs and hands are shaking with excitement. I don't know how to respond to this morning's meeting. Not only did he comfort me yesterday, but today he has defended me in front of the whole company.

-Thank you very much for what you said earlier, Mr. Can.

He smiles at me. I want him to hug me, to assure me that everything is going to be all right.

122

-It's nothing. I would have done the same for any employee.

No, he didn't defend me because I inspire affection in him. I'm sure our conversations in Asmara flowed because we share the same tastes. I would have talked about the same thing with any other employee who was also a literature buff or had traveled to Asmara like me.

-You're not wearing the ring today?

Oh, the damn wedding ring. I take it out of my bag and put it on my finger.

-I'm not used to wearing it in public. I'm very jealous of my private life.

-I'm sorry I intruded then.

-That's all right.

After an awkward silence, I discover my work for today. I have to deliver a report to a friend of Can's who runs an important association.

-It's a secret project parallel to the film. I don't want the spy to find out because we're going to use it to let the public know about us.

-I understand.

I pick up the folder and leave the office. Mr. Emre hasn't asked me for anything and I don't know whether to inform him of this new project. Perhaps it is a secret plan of Can's and it is important that his brother knows about it. However, this time I don't dare betray Can's trust and I start to doubt.

I begin to doubt - is Can really a scoundrel? An evil king who enjoys controlling others? I have never seen him treat anyone badly. On the contrary, he is like a generous gentleman who looks out for others.

I say goodbye to Ceycey and beg him to tell Deren that I've left on Mr. Can's orders, so she won't get angry if she doesn't find me. I head for Can's friend's office. I take a bus and reflect on the changes that have taken place in my life. I am now an ordinary office worker as my parents wished. Long gone are the days when I hardly left my neighborhood unless I went to college. Back then, I entertained myself by running around the street and if I worked, it was for small butcher's orders. I can't believe it. Every time I think about it. The espionage conflicts I get involved in are surreal.

Sometimes I'm glad I didn't discover the albatross. At least for now. If I had to face him and Mr. Can at the same time, I would go crazy. I have mixed feelings about my boss and I'm afraid I can no longer work with Mr. Emre to expose him. I feel increasingly uncomfortable lying to him.

Maybe if I pay him back little by little, I could take this burden off my shoulders. Between Leyla and me, we can pay him back in a year and then I wouldn't have to keep deceiving my family about the butcher's debt.

While I wait for Mr. Can's friend to receive me, I think about whether I should continue writing. I haven't touched my notebook in days. My strange routine has turned my fiction into a vulgarity. I live in a mixture of Kafka novel and teenage romance. Do I really have talent? My inspiration comes only from the majestic albatross. In my imagination it flies free in the company of another bird of great beauty, as in the dream with which I said goodbye to Asmara.

-Good morning, Sanem Aydin?

A gentleman approaches me. He must belong to Can's group. However, he is an office man, one of those who settle down in Istanbul and make a career here.

-Yes, it's me.

-It's a pleasure. My name is Ilhan.

Mr. Ilhan invites me into his office for a cup of tea. He's interested in my work in the studio, perhaps a little too much. Maybe I'm being paranoid, but I sense that Can has told him about me.

-You're a very beautiful girl. Hasn't Can asked you to be an actress?

-Of course not. I'm not cut out for it.

Although hearing the praise has boosted my battered ego a bit. Mr. Ilhan doesn't have to suck up to me. If he praises me, it's because I'm not so useless.

-Did Can tell you about the secret project?

-No. I'm surprised. Why would he trust me with it? I'm just a simple errand girl. Well, actually I was hired as a designer, although I don't have much work now.

-You shouldn't underestimate your talent, Sanem. Can raved about your job interview, and he doesn't usually lavish praise on me.

I blush, but what interests me most is to know if Mr. Ilhan is going to open a recruitment process soon. I wish my bosses were like him. Okay, to be honest, for me to love my job, I'd just have to trade Deren for a nicer supervisor.

-I think you might be interested in this project-, Ilhan continues. -We're going to campaign against discrimination against women in the workplace, and we're going to shoot a commercial and take pictures with models. The aim is to demonstrate the value of women, and it has public funding. Would you be interested in participating?

This confirms that my life is more like a novel than anything I write.

-Why me? I'm not an actress.

-That's where I think your potential lies," Ilhan explains to me. We want to show young girls from the street, the prototype of women that our society doesn't associate with the working world. Your simplicity will make the photos look authentic.

The offer is tempting. In the neighborhood, many women only know the working world if their husbands run a business. The rest spend their days as housewives. For example, my mother helps out in the butcher's shop from time to time and her chores are reduced to housework. She has always encouraged Leyla and me to take charge of our lives. I believe that if I participate in this campaign, my mother will be able to look at me with pride. I will have been part of an important project for many girls who don't know what their future will be.

-You have convinced me, Mr. Ilhan.

Can's friend smiles at me and shakes my hand warmly. I wonder how their friendship came about, how two people with such different lifestyles come to each other without hesitation even as the years go by? Despite slight differences in our tastes, Ayhan and I have shared everything and have always imagined ourselves as neighbors, going to each other's house whenever we seek comfort.

Can, on the other hand, has always traveled from one country to another until now. He will not stay in Istanbul for long. However, Mr. Ilhan will continue to talk to him while I will just remember our little insubstantial conversations.

-I am very glad, Sanem. Since I don't want Can to kill me for stealing one of his employees, what do you say we do a little photo shoot on Friday next week? Can told me that on that day you will participate in a gala party organized by a foreign company. They'll give you the day off, so we won't bother anyone.

-That's perfect-, I say, but suddenly I have a doubt. Mr. Can's not going to the photo shoot, is he?

Ilhan bites his lips. Have I screwed up as usual?

-No. Can has a reputation as a photographer, but he's going to delegate responsibilities. He runs a studio now; he has to focus his attention on the family business.

-I understand.

On one hand, I sigh with relief. On the other, I'm sad not to share an intimate moment with Mr. Can. Stupidity. He thinks I'm engaged and I'm still looking for my fascinating albatross. I shouldn't have to embrace it all. I don't deserve so much happiness.

Mr. Can is kind to me, but all that glitters is not gold.

I say goodbye to Mr. Ilhan and return to the office. I keep my future photo shoot a secret. First of all, because Mr. Can wants this project to be secret. If it leaks out, he will know that I have betrayed him. Facing his disappointed face would break me down. But why am I so upset that he despises me? Emre, Ilhan. They are decent men. They have always been kind to me, have never made fun of me and have trusted me with important tasks. Emre has entrusted me to protect his father's business; Ilhan, to lead a campaign that will help many girls and women who are considering locking themselves in their homes for the rest of their lives.

They deserve my respect. Can has only been supportive at times. He is smart with his choice of words. With him I feel special, protected, valued. That's what they say love is, but love is something more. It is about projecting oneself on the other, about total trust in the loved one, and I don't trust Mr. Can. I dare not ask him if he really wants to sink his father's studio in order to be free.

This doubt prevents love from arising. He inspires only affection in me and this feeling turns to pain when I realize that I value a man who thinks only of himself.

However, he appreciates me. He has spoken of me to one of his childhood friends. There is no need for me to deceive Ilhan. Silence is what inspires those we don't care about and he chose to make me known.

I want to write a poem. One that shows me the truth of what I feel as I reread it. I long for my albatross. If I talk to him, will it all become clear? Will I stop dreaming? Sometimes I ponder whether it would not be better for me if Can were a real albatross and went away from Istanbul to join his beloved.

Only then would my suffering cease.

CHAPTER XV

I try to write at night, but a wall blocks my creativity. That wall has a name: Can Divit.

What could I say about Can Divit? He is the typical protagonist of love stories. Handsome, rich, famous, fascinating, although as in some stories he hides behind his mask of virtue a dark heart. He is not an albatross, but a tiger that devours the little animals that cross his path. He runs through jungles where maidens dare not enter. He flees to the desert, and it is in the heat and aridity that he is comfortable.

In the office, the women talk about him. They all sigh for one of his smiles. They want him to tell them about his travels, to attract their attention so they feel special, a jewel among many ordinary boulders. However, I hear he loves a woman named Polen. She accompanied him to the company's opening party, where my albatross embraced me with her wings. They see each other only a few times a year. However, those occasions will be days of jubilation: the day the albatross travels all the way to the Galapagos.

The day of the photo shoot is approaching. Ilhan has promised me it won't last long. Can has announced to the office that all employees are invited. We will have to dress for the occasion. I will be able to dress up in a ball gown, although I have already shown that such settings are not for me. But what if I meet the albatross again?

I haven't written anything since that distant opening paragraph. The protagonists of the great stories are princesses or peasant women who keep a great talent. I belong to neither group. I'm just a mediocre girl who is fit to work in a butcher shop. I don't stand out among the steaks and sausages. There's nothing that shines about me. Why have I been chosen for an important photo shoot?

I'm a street girl, that's what Mr. Ilhan said.

On the day when I'll pretend I'm a princess again, I'm heading to the first stage. I will be photographed in different settings. The first is an abandoned factory that has been set up for the shoot. Mr. Ilhan accompanies me. He drives me around in his car, as if he were my chauffeur.

I get out of the carriage that life has given me and face the factory. It is a dilapidated building, although what will matter will be its interior. Mr. Ilhan bids me farewell.

-Good luck and enjoy.

It sounds like an incantation. My heart trembles as I enter the ruined palace, inside which a gentleman prepares his weapons: a camera.

And that knight is the one with whom I fantasize about giving him my garment to fight in the tournaments for me.

-Mr. Can! What are you doing here?

He gazes at me as if I were an apparition.

-Sanem, you shouldn't be here. Wait. Are you the model?

I secretly curse Ilhan. She played with me, she lied to me. She's the rope that binds two forces destined to run away from each other.

-Yes, Mr. Ilhan told me you weren't going to be the photographer.

-In the end he insisted that I was. It's a secret project. The fewer people involved, the better. Do I bother you?

That's not what you inspire in me, Can. I love a sweet and kind being. You're a tempest. No one is indifferent to a freak of nature. His muscles show through his T-shirt. He wears a light jacket with rolled up sleeves and in his hands a camera is a wonderful object.

-You'll make me nervous, Mr. Can. I'm not used to this and you....

-What's wrong with me?

He approaches me. He invites me to trust him. I'm your knight, not a monster or an evil king who seeks to dominate you.

-You're my boss. I'm just a simple employee. The one who delivers the coffees...

-You're more than that, Sanem.

Is it true? Is there a jewel hidden in my heart? Do I awaken the attraction of the man who has seen all the treasures of the world?

-You are perfect for the campaign. I hadn't thought of you. However, Ilhan was more inspired.

He holds out his hand. Should I take it? In the end even he realizes the strangeness of the gesture. He pretends he was going to point me to a dressing room to change.

-Please, Sanem. Trust yourself.

But what I want is to trust him.

-All right.

-Well... -I laugh. Now he doesn't know what to do with his outstretched arm. He's pointed too soon. The awkwardness doesn't fit Can Divit, and yet I'm glad he's able to express it. -There are several models. You can change. You're not wearing your ring today?

Why do we always talk about that ring?

-I keep it in my pocket. Because of the photo shoot. Today, it combines less than ever.

-Yes, it's true.

Our conversations have never been so fragile on both sides. We're both afraid of being the one to spoil the magic moment of the session. Hurrying, I dress as a bricklayer. I am now a different Sanem, one who gets up every morning to build her future from sun up to sun down.

-Get over there.

First I pretend to cut some wood. What would I build with it? A throne for Can? A writer's table? No, I won't be a writer. That's not my destiny.

-Perfect, Sanem. Now we have to smile.

Smile?

-You have a beautiful smile. It's dreamy and innocent. Come on. Come on. Dare to show it to the camera.

Every one of his words is a drop that makes happiness bloom on my face. When will this be over? When will we leave for the party?

-Like that. Very good, Sanem-, he congratulates me.

Will anyone recognize me in those pictures?

-Now, get on that crane, please.

I climb up where he tells me to. Can takes a few more shots of me. My hands are shaking. I sweat and slip off the bar I've been holding on to. I shriek and plunge into the void. Only I would break the magic like that. However, Can doesn't let me fall. He picks me up and our eyes connect and we reflect in each other. My heart beats. There is happiness, but also fear.

-Have you hurt yourself?

Never with him. I'm sure of that.

-No.

Shall I ask him to put me down? In literature a moment is eternal. You can reread it and see how it is born and dies again and again. In photography the magic is eternally frozen. I would love to be immortalized. However, there is no one else in this factory but the two of us.

-It's time for us to go to the next stage-, he says, breaking the time that stopped for us. He lowers me down.

-Sure. Besides, we have to go to the gala party. Will that give us time?

132

-Of course. I wasn't counting on you, but we'll be there in the nick of time.

I agree. I change back into my everyday clothes, but I haven't abandoned the story. We climb into Can's SUV and I imagine where the wind and the road will take us.

-You have many hidden talents, Sanem-, Can says to me.

He has opened the windows. The breeze ruffles my hair. Can's mane remains unperturbed, pulled back in his ponytail. How will he be free? Will he be indomitable like his spirit? Soft like his voice?

-You exaggerate.

-I like you better when you call me by my first name.

-You're my boss. I have to keep the manners.

-We're not in the office now. Besides, don't you talk to your colleagues? You're very close to Guliz and Ceycey.

-Are you spying on me?

-No. I care about my employees. It's a small studio and what I hate about Istanbul is that you end up surrounded by nameless faces.

I focus my attention on the scenery outside the window. We approach the pier. Seagulls flutter through the clouds and the air smells of saltpetre. Why do I feel special? Can is not a despotic boss. When he's not locked in his office, he chats with most of my colleagues.

-So you prefer to be called Can?

-Yes.

It is dangerous to create an intimacy between the two of us. I want to write my book about the albatross, a novel about a normal girl who starts working, and yet as I turn the pages of my notebook I hear only this man's laughter.

We park at the dock. Can tells me he's rented a boat and I'll pretend I'm fishing.

-Will we have time to get to the party?

-If you'll allow me a few phone calls, I'll take care of it.

As he finishes setting everything up, I sit on the gangplank of the dock. I go barefoot and my feet brush against the water. The caress transports me to an alternate reality, to the coast of the Galapagos.

-What are you thinking? Inspiring for a story?

-No. I doubt my talent.

-How can you doubt? -Have you finished a novel?

-Not yet. I've only written short stories.

-Well, think about that when you finish it and see how you can improve. I'd love to read a novel by you.

He calls an old fisherman who lends us his boat. Among the tackle I'll use for the session I ponder Can's mood. Would it break my wall if I wrote for him?

On this occasion I pose in a gentle manner. I enjoy casting the net and imagining I've caught a huge fish. Can gazes at me with his camera. I ignore the clicks as the picture is taken. The wind picks up and the boat capsizes. Can pulls me and stops me from falling into the water. Why am I so clumsy? Do I want him to hold me in his arms? His warmth is comforting. Still, this is not a love story, but a simulation. It is a purely professional relationship.

We rest. The boat drifts for a while. Can has put on his sunglasses and gazes at the sky.

-I wish we could catch a fish and roast it-, he says.

-I'd have to be a real fisherwoman to do that.

-No. That takes patience. Prizes don't come overnight.

I blush. The wind has ruffled the skin on my cheeks. It cuts, as if the air possessed nails.

-Shouldn't we go back?

-Don't you like to enjoy the moment?

Fear of answering holds my tongue. Can gazes at me amused. I guess I'll look like an idiot in my yellow raincoat.

The cell phone rings. I startle and Can looks disgusted.

-What do you want Deren?-, he replies. -Yeah, I've got it all worked out. Don't worry about it. Okay, woman, don't get upset. We're on our way. Yes, I'm with Sanem.

No. Why did you tell Deren my name? She hates me enough without her thinking I'm getting too close to Mr. Divit.

-Well, Deren's a little upset. She loves punctuality-, Can continues. It's time for us to go back ashore.

I'm glad. With Ceycey and Güliz I'll be able to camouflage myself among the guests. They are my friends, ordinary people who don't have palaces or a fortune in the bank. Even though we are dressed like rich people... Oh no.

-Can! I don't have a dress for the party! I'm not going as a fisher!

Can's laughter booms over the sea.

-Of course you're not. You'll look prettier than ever today.

Two vans are waiting for us at the dock. What has this man come up with?

-One is for you and one is for me. While we go to the party, a hair and make-up team will prepare you for the party. You have several dresses at your disposal. Choose the one you like the most.

What's Can's problem? Now he wants to become the fairy godmother in the fairy tale?

-Are you serious?

-Of course I am. I would never joke with you. I guess to keep Deren from killing us both, we should get to the party as soon as possible. Don't wait for me.

I'm all for it. It would stir up a lot of gossip in the office if I arrived accompanied to a gala party with Can Divit. I'm sure Arzu Tas would have a fit.

I get into the van with a bit of fear. I need to hold on to something. Inside the vehicle there are three girls, the hairdressers and make-up artists that Can told me about, and a beautiful selection of dresses among which stood out one the color of the petals of a rose in a soft tone.

It is the most beautiful dress I have ever seen in my life. I am not worthy of it. In fact, I'm still wearing the yellow raincoat and my street clothes.

-Welcome, my name is Sila-, the head of my transformation team introduces herself.

-Nice to meet you, I'm Sanem.

My heart is on the verge of fainting. She assures me that when I get out of there I will arrive at the party as the princess of the fairy tale.

CHAPTER XVI

As a child I had read countless fairy tales. One of my favorites was Cinderella. I adored the poor maid who, thanks to her fairy godmother, could enjoy for a few hours a world she did not know.

Would Cinderella tremble before presenting herself to the nobility of the palace? Would she wonder at every moment if she should be there? Would she even think of running away?

I didn't want to look at myself in the mirror Sila held up to me. Not even my mother would recognize me. The partygoers turn around when they see me. It is a cocktail party held in an open-air stone patio. In the distance, the sea is visible. Amidst a sea of faces astonished that I dare to walk around, I recognize some of my colleagues. They stare at me with their mouths open. Actually, I am ashamed that my attire stands out among the others. All the women have chosen discreet dresses and mine stands out like a pale flame in the middle of the night.

-Sanem?

Fate entertains us. It imagines ways to torture us with cruelty. Next to me is Leyla. Days ago she mentioned she had an important social event. It never occurred to me that she meant this party.

-Leyla? What are you doing here?

-The organization has invited members of my company. It's a good networking opportunit-, she explains.- My goodness. You look beautiful!

She really is beautiful. I've always admired my sister's beauty. Her eyes as blue as two sapphires, her pale skin. I'm browner and smaller like my mother. However, Leyla is a goddess. It's only natural that Osman, Ayhan's brother, is in love with her.

-Sanem! Sanem! Where have you been?-, Ceycey asks me, running towards me. He also looks at me as if for the first time. Why am I so happy? -Good heavens, the party is black tie, but your beauty should be forbidden.

-Where did you get that dress? -Güliz intervenes.

Since when does the princess in the fairy tale find herself surrounded by loved ones before dancing with the prince?

-That's what I'd like to know. Even with both of our salaries we couldn't buy it.

I'm ashamed. I turn around. Walking down the stairs leading to the courtyard, Can smiles at me. He defies etiquette in the most outlandish attire. He wears a jacket with medals on it, as if he were a victorious war hero. To me, however, he is a real hero today. I will never be able to thank him for what he has made me feel now.

-I was organizing a secret project with Mr. Can. We got delayed and he lent me this dress.

-Wow, wow. You really climb the corporate ladder. That's my little sister-, Leyla congratulates me.

Suddenly, Ceycey and Güliz wake up from sleep. They introduce themselves to Leyla and I mediate between the three of them. Leyla wins them over immediately, she has always had a talent for winning admiration, although her smile tells me that this is my chance to shine.

-Deren is going to take a picture of you to hang in her room and practice shooting with it-, Güliz whispers to me in a mischievous tone.

I don't dare look at my boss. I don't want to feel intimidated today, so I drink with my friends and Leyla. Some gentlemen approach us. They shiver when I look at them and my sister takes my arm in a protective gesture. Do they want to ask me to dance?

-I love this song!-, Ceycey exclaims. I'm sure he's had a little too much to drink. -Come on, Sanem. Let's dance!

I get carried away and we dance to the music. It's a crazy dance, like Ceycey, but the one I want to dance with most is my prince, my dear albatross. Where is he?

At the end of the song, Can and Deren introduce us to the organizer of the party, an Italian tycoon named Enzo Fabri. I recognize his name because I love the perfumes he produces, so he immediately piques my interest and he seems interested in me. I sense from my dress that he will think I have a similar position in the company to Can or Deren.

-It is a pleasure to meet you all-, says Mr. Fabri. -You have employees to match Can. Your perfume is wonderful, Miss-, he says, turning to me. -What brand is it? I don't recognize it.

-None, sir. It's homemade-, I answer happily. I am thrilled that my perfumes are appreciated. As a child, I even considered going into the world of perfumes. I produce it with different types of flowers and sometimes I experiment. I am very proud of this one. Its scent lingers for a long time, although it doesn't have a very penetrating aroma.

-Wow, Sanem. You look like an expert-, Deren interjects, -although you don't need to bore Mr. Enzo with such details.

-On the contrary, Miss Sanem. I am interested in your knowledge. Do you know my company?

-Of course, Mr. Fabri. You are a world-class reference in the industry and I love your latest products despite the decline in sales. I think the general public was not yet ready for them.

Ceycey and Güliz look at me with their mouths open. Can smiles although his gesture, like Deren's, is also a bit tense and I fear that with my euphoria at meeting Mr. Fabri I have overdone it.

-Wow, Sanem. You don't even know the figures of a big company. How can you compare them?-, Deren says to me, his sibylline eyes fixed on me.

I don't want to embarrass Mr. Can in front of such a high-level sponsor, so I use my photographic memory and my knowledge of perfumes to present Mr. Fabri's sales figures for the last year and compare them with those of his main competitors.

-My God, Sanem. I want to recruit you for my company's executive committee. You have an overflowing talent.

From the look on Deren and Can's faces, you'd think I'd been insulting Mr. Fabri's ancestors.

-Sanem is an indispensable member of our team-, Can interjects with a slight dryness, though he gives Mr. Fabri a warm smile. -You don't want us to start a war over her, do you?

The atmosphere is so tense you could tear it with a knife, though the only one at ease is Mr. Fabri.

-Of course not, Can. Especially now that I want to form an alliance with you. I've heard a rumor that you're preparing a campaign to defend women's rights in the working world.

-Exactly. I see that you don't miss a thing-, Can confesses.

-I'd love to have our company's image associated with yours. So the only favor I ask is that you allow me to steal Sanem for a dance.

Mr. Fabri? One of the most important businessmen in the world wants to dance with me?

-I think the only one who has the right to decide about it is Sanem-, Can says, looking me in the eyes without smiling.

-Of course I will be happy to dance with you, Mr. Fabri-, I reply. Hopefully this is a good decision and I won't have to regret it.

I head with Mr. Fabri to the dance floor. Now I really am Cinderella dancing with the prince, although magic should permeate my dance. This is my fairy tale and I feel out of place.

I watch Can, who gazes at me leaning on a balustrade. He is no longer a knight, no longer a hero. Just a despot king who asks his maid why she dances with a foreign prince. He does not smile at me, though he does not hate me. His fury is directed at Mr. Fabri.

Can is unrecognizable. A dark area surrounds him now. Is it that character that pushes him to betray his brother? As I dance I look for Leyla with my eyes. I hope she won't tell our parents anything, although she is distracted talking to Mr. Emre. He looks at me suspiciously, too. Does he know I've been involved in Can's project? From what Mr. Fabri explained, that campaign is what pushed him to sign a business agreement with the studio. I am sure that we will now have the funds to shoot a wonderful film. I am responsible for that, for giving wings to Can's obscurity.

I think of myself, the fishwife-turned-princess who writes her story with trembling steps. In every fairy tale there are dark woods and a voice that whispers and tempts us into danger. Evil kings invite us with their charm to dangerous adventures. The princesses accept even though they know they will be heartbroken as soon as they enter the forest. Who am I in this story? Am I going to accept what my destiny dictates? Or follow the evil king and wait for him to break my heart?

Can seems to want to answer those questions. He turns to me, his useless subject, and takes me by the hand and separates me from Mr. Fabri. My evil king pulls me out of the party. I look at the sky for a second. There is no sign of the albatross and for a second I am glad. Can has completely overturned my heart.

-What's wrong with you, Can?

I forget that he's my boss, and that I'm only the princess because he wanted me to be.

-That man shouldn't treat you like that, like you're a doll he can use as he pleases.

-It was nothing, Can.

It's true that for a moment Mr. Fabri looked at me as if he wanted me to be his princess. He didn't even kiss my hand.

— I'm sorry, Sanem. I have gone too far, but as I told you I care about my employees-, he says. Where did the king who feared nothing go?

-Thank you, Can, but I can take care of myself.

-I know.

He's sorry. The confident Can Divit has acted out of an outburst and he's ashamed of it.

-I'm going to leave. I don't feel comfortable. I'm not really cut out for parties. I don't know what I was thinking putting this on.

In the end, playing Cinderella comes with consequences. I'm not cut out for balls in a palace by the sea.

-I'm suffocated by these damn formalities too-, he admits. Everyone looks at me funny for not wearing a tuxedo. They think I'm an eccentric.

-And isn't that true?

I get emboldened. I still feel the warmth of Can's hand on my skin.

-Let's go-, he says then, with a smile that encourages me to be braver.

-But what about the others? What about the appointment with Mr. Fabri?

-I care more about you, Sanem.

He holds out his hand to me again.

-Would you like to eat a nice plate of meat?

That was the strangest request in the world, yet on Can's lips it was worthy of appearing in even the most beautiful love story.

I accept his offer and intertwine my fingers with his. We run. I don't know where to. Back to the vans? Are we going by bus looking like this?

I don't fly with the albatross, I run with a tiger that would never hurt me. Its claws don't dig into my skin, but rather give me strength and self-confidence.

I feel that I am moving forward in the midst of a dream and that, at the least expected moment, dawn will snatch this gift from me. Can Divit gives up to no one, though. If he wished, Morpheus himself would allow him to remain in my dreams forever.

The pity is that this is not the story I desire. I do not know what tale I am writing, but if I have one certainty it is that Can is only a fickle spirit like the wind and that he will disappear when the pages of my story become boring to him.

CHAPTER XVII

Can drives through the mountain. We are on the outskirts of Istanbul, in a mysterious place. I'm still wearing my princess costume. My clothes are in a backpack in the trunk of the SUV.

The phones are ringing off the hook. I pick up mine. It's Leyla.

-What a pain in the ass. You can't enjoy a good plate of meat like that.

-Did something happen with Mr. Fabri?

I'm beginning to suspect that it wasn't a good idea for me to leave the party, taking Mr. Can with me.

-Surely, but our workday is over and I'm starving. Shall we turn off the phones?

I agree. The silence calms me down. Now only Can is with me and the only thing that will distract us will be the music on the radio and the other's voice.

-Where are we going?

-To my secret refuge-, Can answers, enigmatic.

The place where Can hides from the rest of the world is a small hut in the middle of the forest. I hear the birds singing and the breeze whispering to the leaves of the trees.

-I think you'd better change.

He leads me to the cabin. It has only one room that functions as a bedroom, dining room and kitchen. He closes the doors to preserve my privacy and, as I change, Mr. Emre's ring falls to the floor.

I pick it up. It is the symbol of a lie: of a marriage that will never happen except in Can's imagination, though it offers me some protection. I put it on my finger and cling to the story I've created around it.

I am going to get married. I'm just an employee who has created a close relationship with her boss.

I walk out of the cabin. Can has shed his jacket and is chopping wood with an axe. His abs are marked as he splits the wood. His gaze flicks to my ring. Then he focuses on me, scrutinizing me.

We don't speak while Can lights the fire. Then we resume the conversation, though all we're interested in is meat. I explain my favorite way to cook meat, though I'm only an expert in theory; in practice there's no one more disastrous at cooking than I am.

-Would you like to drink some wine? I keep a very good one here for a roast.

-I'd love some.

I notice that the fridge has plenty of supplies, that there are books with bookmarks on the kitchen table, and that there's not a trace of dust on any of the cabin furniture.

-Do you come here often?

-Yes. When I need to get away from the city, nature relaxes me. It reminds me a bit of my travels.

With food, the wine loosens our tongues a little more and spurs our spirits. A flame runs through my mood. I joke with Can and call him a presumptuous artist and ask for a dance.

-We should have a song, don't you think?

I agree. I get up and head for a shelf full of music records. I move around the cabin like it's my second home, too.

-I love rock! -I squeal. I don't feel like romantic palace songs anymore.

For a second I dance alone, unleashed, until Can picks me up in his arms and lifts me up, spinning me around. Because of the wine, I seem to have lost my way in the middle of a hurricane.

-Can, stop. Please.

His finger brushes against my ring. The gigantic gem that adorns it is capable of cutting his skin. Gently, he sits me on a log and encourages me to eat some more meat. I devour it. I am the hungriest beast in Turkey.

-You are unrecognizable, Sanem.

-You really don't know me, Can Divit-, I tell the smug man. -We both lie to each other. What don't you tell me?

I sit up and turn around. I start a new crazy dance. Can whispers in my ear.

-Sanem, don't drink any more wine.

It's so sweet and warm. I snuggle against his chest, wrap my arms around him. Can is as big as my albatross.

-You don't order me around. I'm getting married.

There's got to be a silver lining to lying, right? Actually, we shouldn't hug. We're both committed to one person, even if in my case it's just another lie.

-Sanem-, Can says to me. Their lips are very close.

-Yes, Can?

I close my eyes. For a moment I dream that he confesses that he is my albatross and kisses me. However, all that happens is that I give in to tiredness and fall asleep, safe next to Can.

I wake up. I stretch and curse whoever hit my head with a hammer. I scratch and scratch myself with the stone of my engagement ring. Even though I wear it every time I have to face Can Divit, I can't get used to it. I have tried many times to return it to Mr. Emre, but he insists that I must still maintain the alibi I invented to justify my raid on Can's house.

I sit back up and discover that I have slept in the bed in the cabin, wrapped in soft sheets. My goodness, what time is it? I look at my wristwatch. It's nine o'clock, and since it can't possibly be night because the sun is shining brightly, that means I've slept in the cabin with Can and my parents are going to kill me when I get home.

-Good morning, Sanem.

Can leans against the door frame. He drinks a cup of tea. He looks fresh as a daisy, though I sense he has nursed me through my alcoholic convalescence. I wobble and Can offers me his arm for support.

-What happened?

My boss smiles, nervously I'd say.

-It's a simple summary. We ate and I served you wine. We played music, danced and you kept drinking more. I wanted to stop you, but it was impossible to control you.

Oh, my God. Can is silent about something. I try to force my memory, but I can't remember anything.

-Mr. Can, was I out of line last night?

-You don't have to worry about anything.

On the contrary, my mother is going to put me away for life. I pull out my cell phone and proceed to count my mother's missed calls. I'm surprised to discover that Leyla is the only one who tried to contact me yesterday. I suspect she has my back.

-I must get home.

-Of course.

I walk leaning my weight on Can. I pray that the effects of my hangover will wear off before I get home. My boss barely speaks. I'm grateful because my headache is getting worse. We leave the mountain and head back to town.

-You can drop me off here. You don't have to go into the neighbor-hood.

-No way, Sanem. You're barely on your feet.

-Okay-, I agree, not having the strength to rebel.

I pick up my cell phone and call Leyla. My sister answers right away and her voice adds to my headache.

-Sanem, where are you!

-I'm coming home, Leyla-, I mumble like a zombie. I- spent the night with Can Divit.

-What? -my sister exclaims. Can hears her too and turns to me, sur-prised.

Understanding how my words can be interpreted, I redden to the roots of my hair.

-No, not in that way. Leyla, who do you think I am?

-I don't know, sis. First you come to a company party in a designer dress that will cost more than our butcher shop. Then you dance with an Italian tycoon and, later, you leave holding Can Divit's hand, you disa-ppear and don't show any sign of life.

-Okay, okay, I left to return the dress, we were drinking and...-, Come on, Sanem, you have to admit it. If you don't, mom and Leyla will whis-per among themselves and make up the most bizarre story-... I drank more wine than I should have and I fell down round. Mr. Can was taking care of me.

Leyla bursts out laughing. I know her well enough to know that the only thing that amuses her is that she's not pulling her hair out.

-You owe me one, Sanem. Yesterday I told Mom you had to go on an urgent business trip and you were coming home today. If you come home reeking of alcohol.

I smell my clothes. I sniff and sniff for a telltale trace.

-I keep mints in my glove compartment-, Can offers.

-Are you coming home with your boss? -asks my sister at the sound of his voice.

-Yes, I'm feeling a bit under the weather-, I reply as I eat a mint.

I don't want to look at Can, under what circumstances have I breathed on him, or do I stink so much that he smells it from where he is?

-Sanem, I'm going to kill you.

I'm thankful today is the weekend and there's no office to go to. I'll lock myself in my room and sleep until I forget last night's nonsense. I say goodbye to Leyla and remain silent until Mr. Can parks at the front door.

Mom is out in the blink of an eye. She must live glued to the window every time I'm outside.

-Good morning, Sanem! Oh, Mr. Can! How nice to see you again.

-It's always a pleasure to visit you, Mevkibe.

-Come in, come in, please. We can treat you to some tea.

I get out of the car with as much dignity as I can muster. I don't speak to throw Can out, because I'm afraid Mom will discover the hangover that's tormenting me.

-I'd love to.

Luckily, Mom pays more attention to Can than to me. I wave at her, pretending I'm feeling great and she doesn't suspect a thing. Maybe I'll rethink going into acting.

The only one who pounces on me, as Dad shakes Can's hand like he's the president, is Leyla. She hugs me, gives me two kisses and whispers in my ear.

-You're dead.

I imagine how, in the middle of the night, they throw my body into the dock. But Leyla and I are the perfect sisters. I lean my head on her shoulder and we walk together. Thanks to that, I can keep a steady pace. While our parents and Can chat at the table, Leyla settles me in the arm-chair and offers me a tea.

I drink it slowly. I savor it. My head improves because the cup is at the perfect temperature, very hot. And, recovering, I realize what it takes to have my parents talking to my boss as if they've known each other all their lives.

-Sanem is a model employee. In fact, she's going to be known all over the country soon because she's starring in a very important project.

Maybe Leyla will lend me her hitman to get rid of Can.

-No way. What project is that?-, Dad is interested.

-It's nonsense, Dad. Mr. Can is exaggerating-, I say, getting up.

I've relied too much on the infusion. I haven't fully recovered, so I stumble and drop the hot tea on my sister's feet. Leyla says nothing, but her face is clear as spring water.

Now she's going to give me a cold water bath and plunge my head all the way in.

-Oh, Sanem, you're so clumsy-, Mom interjects.

-Sanem worked very hard yesterday and we hardly slept last night. I think she should go to sleep-, says Can. The bastard could have started there.

-You must be tired too. You should go home. Thanks for the ride.

-You're welcome.

Can finishes his tea. Leyla has decided to stop being my support. Partly because she has gone to wipe her feet. I say goodbye to Can and head to my room, slowly, but not stopping before Mom catches me off guard.

Luckily. This time, thanks to Leyla, they think I've been an exemplary girl and only comment among themselves about Can's goodness.

-What a handsome, well-mannered man-, I hear my mother say from the stairs. -He is perfect.

When I go to bed after pulling down the blinds, I couldn't agree more with my mother.

Can is too perfect. He would never look at a girl like me.

CHAPTER XVIII

The weekend has been a haven of peace and quiet. For two days I have avoided Can. In return, I have become Leyla's slave until my hair turns gray.

Yesterday I met Ayhan. We spent hours talking about the party and Mr. Can. My friend's eyes sparkled, but she didn't say anything. She just listened to me, even though I know she misunderstood what happened between the two of us. It's not her fault. In truth, the way Can and I left the party gives rise to many misunderstandings. I'm afraid to go to the office today. Güliz and Ceycey will bombard me with questions about what happened. On Friday they both called me on my cell phone and I have ignored them out of embarrassment. My goodness, what a day ahead.

In the studio, I walk around wanting to be unnoticed, though I arouse murmurs wherever I go. I settle in at my desk. With any luck, if I pretend to be focused on a design, Deren forgets about me.

-Blessed are the eyes that see you, Sanem-, Güliz greets me mischievously.

I'm going to have to explain everything to her in detail. I hope she doesn't come to the same conclusions as Ayhan. Although she hasn't confessed it, I know she thinks there's an affair between me and Can.

-Good morning, Güliz. I'm sorry I haven't returned your calls, but I was feeling terrible over the weekend.

-I can't imagine your suffering.

I shut up. My friend lurks, waiting for a sign of weakness to get the truth out of me.

-What did you do at the end of the party?

-Well, since we had worked on the secret project, we didn't eat, so we went for a drink and then he took me home.

Without going into details it sounds like what it is: a normal activity between two co-workers who like each other. That's the key to success.

-Well, if you want me to tell you the truth, when Mr. Can took you by the hand and led you away from Mr. Fabri, I thought I was in the middle of a movie. I was surprised because everybody knows that Mr. Can loves his girlfriend, Miss Polen, very much, but if you say that nothing happened between you?

Güliz is a master in the art of gossip. She wants to get more information out of me, but what she has succeeded in doing is to remind me of reality. Mr. Can is in love with a woman of his class. All he does is treat me well, but if he's really in love with his girlfriend, he shouldn't have taken me out of the party. Now at the office, they'll think I'm a freeloader who wants to break up a relationship. I'm sure Deren will think I'm trying to climb the corporate ladder by seducing Mr. Can. That's why she hates me so much.

I'm useless. I don't deserve this. Mr. Emre is right: Can plays games with others to achieve his goals.

A burning fury rises in my chest and I clench my fists.

-Well, Sanem, you know I'm joking, don't you?

I nod my head and try my best to smile at her. She's not responsible for Can being a scoundrel.

-I wanted to warn you that on Friday we almost lost the contract the studio was going to sign with Mr. Fabri because of Can. Deren was screeching that she was going to fire you, so Ceycey....

My heart stopped. Ceycey had had a few too many drinks at parties and alcohol and my friend are a bad combination for his uncontrollable tongue.

-You see, he said that Mr. Can was jealous of Mr. Fabri's treatment of you because... because you're a couple.

-Ceycey did what?!-, I squeal, attracting all eyes. A wave of murmurs breaks out. My fellow hyenas are about to feast on gossip at my expense.

-Sanem, calm down. He is now explaining it to Mr. Can. Look.

As my scoundrel of a boss's office has glass walls, I watch Ceycey shiver as Deren and Can argue. My predatory boss paces around his desk fussing and occasionally points at my friend, saying something that I'm sure won't be half as fierce as what Ceycey will hear when he talks to him.

-He saved a million-dollar deal, but I feel sorry for the poor guy-, Güliz whispers in my ear. -You and Can are going to tear him apart.

Ceycey comes out of the office accompanied by Deren.

-Sanem, Mr. Can wants to see you!-, Deren shouts at me.

I don't answer her because I pierce Ceycey with my eyes. My traitor of a friend flees to the cafeteria rather than dare to cross me.

-Good luck, Sanem-, Güliz says goodbye.

-Thank you-, I mumble angrily, organizing the words I'm going to say to Can.

People turn away from me as I walk to my boss's office. I enter like a raging bull, ramming the door, which closes on its own from the effect of the impact.

-Sanem, Mr. Fabri is meeting me in five minutes. They told him...

-I know what they told him, Mr. Can!-, I shout. -You should have respected my wish to dance with Mr. Fabri and now the whole office is whispering about us!

-For God's sake, Sanem. They know it's a set-up.

-I will not lie, sir. Face the consequences of your actions.

That said, I take Mr. Emre's ring, which I always keep in my purse, put it on my finger and angrily show it to him.

-Now you're taking out the ring?-, the scoundrel reproaches me.

-I wear it whenever I want because it's my decision! I'm engaged, Mr. Can! And I love my fiancé with all my heart! That's why I won't lie to anyone for you!

-Ah, yes? Well, I don't understand you, Sanem, because you only take him out to use it as a shield.

-I use it as a shield? Against what, may I ask?

Can should thank me for controlling my anger. If I were Mom, I would have stamped a wad of folders on his model head.

-You know perfectly well! I don't understand you! First about Arzu Tas and then about Friday! And you're engaged and you love your boyfriend, but you're looking for your albatross! What do you really want, Sanem?!

I approach him. Such a bastard. Why is he meddling in my affairs? I raise my hand to him. I'll regret it for the rest of my life, but I'll let off steam by slapping him.

-Wow, wow. What a passionate affair. Please, I want to apologize for what happened on Friday. I hope I'm not the cause of your argument.

Can and I both blanch. My hand lingers in the air and Can immediately grabs it with false gentleness.

-My God, what a beautiful ring. Are you engaged? I wish I had known sooner, Miss Sanem. I'm sorry for my manners.

I turn pale. Oh, no. While we were squealing at each other, we didn't realize the whole office was watching. And now the attention falls on my ring, which with that rock is visible from miles away.

-I'm sorry you witnessed our discussion, Mr. Fabri. Sometimes we get out of control of our feelings, but I love Sanem with all my heart.

He hugs me around the waist. My greatest wish is to kill him slowly, cooking him in a pot. However, I smile at Mr. Fabri.

-We were arguing about something silly, sir-, I interject. -My temper is sometimes horrible. I inherited it from my mother.

-I hope it gets better. When did you two get engaged?

-Friday-, Can said, before I could get a word in edgewise. -I was going to ask her that day at dinner, but....

-I'm sorry, please. Don't give me any more explanations. I'm sorry to have been a bone of contention at such a special time. As compensation, I would like your company to take part in a social event. It helps to strengthen team bonding and I'm sure it will help you to unwind. Besides, we can have dinner together one of these evenings.

-It would be a pleasure, Mr. Fabri, wouldn't it, Sanem?

-Nothing would please me more than for all of us to have dinner together-, I reply, smiling even wider. Seriously, now I'm sure that, if I become an actress, I'm capable of winning the Oscar.

-Well, that's it. I'll leave you to settle your differences. Can, we'll sign the contracts tomorrow.

Mr. Fabri leaves and Deren escorts him out. I separate from Can the instant I lose sight of Fabri.

-Are you crazy?-, I whisper. From here, I can see how the others are still gossiping from their desks, even though they pretend to be concentrating on their work.

-What did you want me to do? Tell him that our engagement is a lie and that I pushed you away because I didn't respect your space?

-What do you care what I talked to him about? He's a polite and gallant man. No, like...

-Brother.

We turned around. Mr. Emre has come without us noticing his presence.

-What is it, Emre?

-Did you sign the agreement with Mr. Fabri?

-Yes, we finally settled our differences.

-I'm glad. What a scene you made the other day. You shouldn't burden Sanem so much.

-You don't need to worry about me, Mr. Emre-, although I'm grateful that he does look after me. -I'll adapt to whatever I am told.

I bid them both farewell and return to my desk, ring on my finger. I am already the main reason for this company's gossip.

-Sanem!-, exclaims Güliz, running up to me. -What's with the ring?

-I'm engaged-, I shout. -To a boy from my neighborhood.

Ceycey runs, too. He's kept a safe distance so I won't pounce on him, though he's overheard the conversation with my friend.

-My God, you're engaged! Why didn't you tell us?

I glare at him and, wisely, Ceycey backs away.

-I'm very jealous of my private life. Although now I'm engaged to Mr. Can because someone is very chatty when he has a few too many drinks. Do you know who might have told Mr. Fabri about me, Ceycey?

I have a pen in my hand and I grip it like a dagger. I have rarely proven myself worthy of my mother's daughter, but today the rage is overflowing.

-I'm so sorry, Sanem. I will make it up to you. I promise-, Ceycey assures me.

The things you have to do to save your own skin.

Luckily for my friend, our companions surround us and, upon seeing the ring, and explaining the lie that Mr. Emre designed just for Can, they

158

all now believe that I am engaged and congratulate me.

-Best of all, if you bring it to the cohabitation camp, we can meet him-, Ceycey points out. I turn my head slowly toward him and he gets the message that he hasn't learned to keep his mouth shut.

-Bring him to camp, Sanem-, says Can, who, like the snake he is, has taken advantage of the crowd to creep toward me discreetly. -I'd love to meet your fiancé and apologize to him for involving you in the pantomime with Mr. Fabri.

-Of course, Mr. Can.

When normality returns to the office, I drop my head on the notes on the desk. I fantasize a thousand different ways to assassinate both Can Divit and Ceycey at the same time.

-Wait, tell me again the mess you got yourself into, Sanem-, Leyla asks me, perplexed.

-And why do you need my brother?-, Ayhan also let go.

Oh, my lord. My life is a soap opera.

-Let's see, it's simple. A colleague in the office is a busybody and, so that my company wouldn't lose the contract I was going to sign with Mr. Fabri after Mr. Can's performance, he told Fabri that Can and I were a couple-, I repeat for the umpteenth time, although this time I didn't get the names mixed up.

-What's with the ring?-, Leyla rebukes me, squinting her eyes.

-It's Mr. Emre's. I'm keeping it for him because of a favor he asked me, and when I got nervous with my boss about Ceycey's lie, I put it on my finger and said I wasn't going to lie to him because I was engaged.

-A very logical and mature decision-, Leyla and Ayhan chorused.

-Well, yes, it wasn't my best idea-, I admit. I start sweating. I'd better not tell them that I got upset at Can for getting too confident with me, while having a girlfriend. -The problem is that Mr. Fabri walked into Can's office when I was wearing the ring on my finger and thought we were engaged and, of course, in order not to lose the contract, my boss went along with him and now we have to pretend we're engaged at a cohabitation camp. And you can bring people along and since I don't want them to think I'm a lizard in the company, I also told them that I'm engaged and they all want to meet my real fiancé.

Leyla bursts out laughing and almost chokes on her tea. We are in a neighborhood coffee shop.

-Well, Leyla, I can't tell my boss that I lied to him so he would leave me alone and stay out of my life, but now he wants to meet my fiancé too, and if the three of us talk to your brother, Ayhan, he can....

-Do you want to drag Osman into this mess? He's going to kill us-, my friend assures me.

-Leyla, please ask him too. It's essential that all three of us go.

Ayhan kicks me under the table. She is aware of my plan, but I am desperate and kick her back. My friend doesn't like my sister because Osman has been in love with her all his life and doesn't dare to propose. The poor guy only has eyes for Leyla, even though there are countless girls pining for him in the butcher shop. If she asks him for a favor, he would lack the time to grant it. Although Leyla has never taken advantage of that. She values Osman. However, she is not in love with him.

-Let's see what kind of trouble you get me into too, Sanem. Alright. I'll go with you to talk to Osman, but since he's a piece of bread, I don't think it's necessary. If I help you, it's because I don't want you to get fired owing money to Mr. Emre.

-Thank you very much, Leyla. You are the best sister in the world.

Ayhan, will you talk to Osman too?

She rolls her eyes.

-Okay, but I'm doing it because I don't want to miss his face when you tell him the story. Let's see, in one day you'll have to pretend you're engaged to your boss and my brother at the same time. Only Misifú would have to go to the camp-, she exclaims, laughing. Leyla imitates her. For once, they look like bosom buddies. Too bad it's at my expense. -You'd have three fiancés in one day!

I click my tongue. I put up with being the target of Ayhan and Leyla's mockery because I have no choice. Although I am aware that my story is so surreal that people would only believe it if they read it in the novel. At least I've managed to sneak in the ring without Leyla discovering that I'm also in the middle of a conflict between members of one of Turkey's most influential families.

Eventually, if I run out of ideas, I'll get around to writing this. It's sure to sell like gangbusters as a humor novel.

CHAPTER XIX

Osman is one of the loveliest men I know. Leyla was right. When he heard the story I made up to justify my entanglement, he consoled me and assured me that he would accompany me to camp. My sister didn't have to beg him.

Although now I don't enjoy camp for fear that Can will run into Osman. Who knows what he tells him if I'm not in front of him. We are competing the girls in the office to a game of tug-of-war against the female staff of a rival staff. Ceycey has been tasked with overseeing the activities and is happier than a kid with new shoes.

-Sanem, focus-, Güliz pleads with me.

-Yes, sorry.

Osman is late. I am dragged and my fingers slip on the rope, but my interest is in finding my friend. He and Ayhan have asked Misifu for a car. They finally convinced him because they told him they needed it to do me a favor, though I'm sure he'll be running around now, imagining what kind of mess I've gotten myself into. Well, now I mustn't think about Misifu and the obsessive love he feels for me.

As is evident, in the end we fall down and I get my clothes full of wardrobe. I curse under my breath, although Güliz manages to worsen the state of my nerves.

-My God, who is that hottie with Mr. Can?

I turn to where they're all pointing. Can is walking with Osman. Of course he is. Luck never gives me a break. I run towards them, arousing whispers. However, as I hug Osman and the two of us walk around together, all I care about is warning him.

-You were talking to my boss-, I whisper in his ear.

I cover him with kisses. Since we've known each other since we were kids, he won't mind as long as I don't kiss him on the lips.

-Oh, Osman, I'm so glad you're here, my love!

Can's face is one of total disbelief. Ah, revenge is a delicious and very sweet dish.

-What a welcome, Sanem,-, he replies warmly. The good thing about Osman is that trust flows between us and it's easier to pretend.

I return to my companions holding Osman's hand and introduce him. They look him up and down and I know that Güliz, at least, is envious. Osman should take more advantage of how handsome he is.

For the next few games, I find myself at ease with Osman and deliberately avoid Can. Even in a game that involves guessing company mates, I refuse to say his name even though I recognize his beard and body odor. For a second, my heart falters. Because of his beard, for a second I mistook him for the albatross. However, then I recognize him and turn away from him. I don't want that man to confuse me any more times.

At lunchtime, I enjoy some peace and quiet, as Osman and I eat at a separate table from where we can observe all the camp participants.

-You keep looking at him-, Osman suddenly blurts out.

-At whom?

-Your boss. We've known each other since we were kids. You've never been able to hide anything from me, Sanem. You're my other little sister.

Talking to Osman is reassuring. He doesn't know what evil is and has always supported me in everything.

-If you don't confess your feelings they pile up and hurt. If you don't tell him how you feel, you will constantly regret it.

Osman holds my hand and caresses me. Unlike Ayhan, I know he knows firsthand how I feel.

-Does the voice of experience speak? Would you dare to confess at the same time as me?

We laugh together. Fear makes my voice tremble, though I am not ashamed with Osman. I'm glad he's my friend and not my fiancé. I don't want to lose the relationship I have with him.

-Now Leyla is at an unattainable level. She is very focused on her work. Sooner or later her profession will take her out of Turkey and I am just a grocery store owner.

-You are one of the most wonderful and attractive men I have ever met-, I assure him. —The girl who rejects you because she thinks you're not up to her standards is an idiot.

-We both seem to have a hard time appreciating each other-, he confides, believing my words. -You're more amazing than you think, too.

I have cried at this meal what I have not allowed myself to cry in quite some time. I kiss Osman goodbye with a kiss on the cheek and, as Mr. Fabri is coming for tea, I approach Can to pretend we are engaged.

Despite what I have discussed with Osman, fear seizes my muscles as Can has slipped his arm over my shoulders. We feign cordiality in our words, though there is no point of comparison in this performance as the one I performed with Osman, where it cost me nothing to snuggle up to him. However, Fabri doesn't suspect anything and when he says goodbye he wishes us luck in our relationship.

I am overwhelmed to be next to Can. I want to talk to him, but no one grants me the intimacy I enjoyed with Osman. There is no corner where we can hide.

-Yesterday Ilhan showed me the campaign set-up. In two days, your face will be on posters all over Turkey. I have a copy here. Do you want it?

How different it was to take the photos. Now I receive them with anguish. This man baffles me. His actions prompt me to think he cares more about me than he wants to admit. However, he has a girlfriend. It's not a set-up like mine with Osman. Why must he always be as tempestuous and unpredictable as a force of nature?

I say goodbye to him with hardly any more words. On a terrace Mr. Emre is having a cup of coffee. I approach his table and he immediately offers me a seat next to him.

-Good afternoon, Sanem, is he really your boyfriend?-, he asks, looking at Osman, who is busy talking to Güliz and Ceycey.

-No, he's a childhood friend. I had a hard time coming up with a story to justify the ring without mentioning anything about its relation with Mr. Can.

-I appreciate your discretion, Sanem. I'm surprised you're handling this situation so well.

-I'm not, Mr. Emre. I get tired of lying to everyone. I just want to know when I can return the ring to you.

Emre takes a sip of coffee and meditates. He looks at the envelope with the photos. I've left it on the table. I don't dare look at the photos and remember what I experienced with Can.

-Now that the office believes in your commitment, we should wait a little longer. Luckily, thanks to your friend, people won't ask any more questions. Or is something else bothering you, Sanem?

I can't explain to him that I'm starting to doubt Can. He will stop trusting me.

-These photos are the ones Can took of me for the campaign he's going to advertise. In the end, I didn't manage to foil the deal with Mr. Fabri. I'm a disaster.

Mr. Emre holds my hands. For a second, he looks around and looks worried. I think he has seen someone. All that's missing now is for them to whisper about my relationship with Emre as well.

-Sanem, don't worry. My brother used you for his plans. Actually, I never imagined he would come up with something like this to seduce Fabri. I'm sure he pulled strings to make sure he found out shortly before the party. My brother is an artist when it comes to achieving his goals.

He is right. However, why does my heart whisper to me that I am special to Can?

-Keep the photos, Mr. Emre. I don't want them.

-Alright.

I say goodbye to him and walk around the camp pondering my feelings. I move forward like a wanderer who wants to return home and can't find the right way. Without realizing it, I bump into a woman. She is the owner of a rival company. I think Deren and her don't have a good relationship because in the games they kept giving each other murderous looks.

-I'm sorry.

-It's all right. I'm Aylin Yüksel.

I finally recognize the name. She's the woman whose company has benefited from the leaks of the Divits' projects.

-I'm Sanem Aydin. It's a pleasure to meet you.

-Don't think so. It's my pleasure-, she answers me enigmatically, though I can see the coldness in her perfect smile.

We say goodbye, although the bad vibes from my encounter with Aydin still linger. She doesn't detest me like Arzu or Deren, but I've never felt so worried about the reaction I've caused in someone else.

Determined not to add any more burdens to my list of problems, I return to my friends and Osman. At least there is little left for this frustrating day to come to an end.

CHAPTER XX

I fiddle with the pen. In front of me is a blank sheet of paper. Osman is not lying when he says that unexpressed feelings build up inside and hurt. They are like acid that devours flesh. Yet I can't write another line. Can, my albatross. They both flit through my head and sometimes I dream of them both. Sometimes Can even transforms into the majestic bird and offers me to fly on his wings.

After camp, I spoke with Ayhan. She approves of her brother's every word. Returning with Osman in the car, I encouraged him to be bolder with my brother, but he kept quiet. No words of love came from his lips, just as ink does not flow from my pen.

I become overwhelmed. I look out the window. The moon has grown fatter these nights and now looks completely full over my house. I wonder if Can is watching the sky. I have made up my mind. Tomorrow is the weekend, I will go to my boss's house and talk to him. I will tell him the truth, at least the only truth I need to express: my love for him. For Can, I am able to ignore the albatross. A month has passed. It's funny how time marches on. I think I've been at work forever because of how fast the projects are moving. We're shooting a romance film, I've met many famous actors, and yet I still haven't found my albatross. Maybe it wasn't an employee of the company, but someone who crashed the party uninvited. I don't care anymore, I just want to talk to Can Divit and convey my feelings to him, although I don't know what will happen next. Will he respond to my love? Will he ignore me?

I understand why Osman does not dare to talk to Leyla about his feelings. Taking the first step is complicated. Moving forward, it is impossible to go back and return to the starting point. However, fear is the enemy of love. What makes it impossible for me to talk to Can has destroyed our relationship. The other night I had dinner with him and Mr. Fabri, as we had agreed, and although we made up a thousand anecdotes for a love story, the connection between us is gone.

The day on which I will confess my feelings to Can Divit dawns sunny. It seems a good omen. I shower, eat breakfast and say goodbye to my family. My parents are relaxing watching a movie with Leyla. For them, the romance has worked. They have raised my sister and me with love. They are proof that love exists.

I think about that as I take the bus to visit Can. The trip seems to take forever and the final destination, terrible. In romances, it's always the man who declares himself to his beloved. I wish Can would come to my house with a bouquet of roses to propose, but I live in reality and I have to take responsibility for how I feel. I can't take it anymore. I'm not going to keep quiet. I will tell him that with him I feel protected, inspired. That I am afraid to meet him and yet I want him to share his concerns with me.

Calling his house, I repeat my statement over and over again, although with each attempt I change the fundamental phrase. Can is surprised by my visit. Before he says anything, I step forward and look him in the eye.

-Good morning, Can. Sorry for coming unannounced, but there was something I wanted to tell you.

-It's all right, Sanem. Come in and we'll talk.

There's a special gleam in his eye. He notices my hands and notices that my engagement ring is missing. He smiles at me and the bond between us reappears. Does he really love me?

We settle into an armchair in the dining room. In the movies, confessing feelings is simple. Music accompanies the scene, which flows naturally. However, my voice cracks. Please, Can, discover my love in my expression, in my hands trembling from wanting to caress you and not finding the necessary courage.

-Are you all right, Sanem? Is it because of the campaign? Do you want us to take down the photos?

The day before yesterday the campaign started. At first I was surprised to see my face on billboards, but I'm used to it now, especially because of the pride my parents felt when they found out what kind of campaign I was involved in.

-Please, not that. Thank you very much for letting me participate. What I want to tell you is...

Can's cell phone rings. Without hesitation, he turns it off. The only one he wants to talk to is me. Come on, that should cheer me up, spur my heart to guide my lips. Maybe if I kiss him, everything is easier. Or worse. Since when does the girl make the first move?

-What do you want to tell me, Sanem?-, He guides me with infinite gentleness. He offers me his hands for me to take them and take refuge in his warm touch.

-You see, Can, it's complicated....

-It doesn't matter.

The phone interrupts us again. This time, Can turns it off.

-My brother has always been very inconvenient-, he jokes. I manage to smile with him. -Now, Sanem, take your time. You don't have to tell me everything now. Talk when you feel comfortable. There's no rush.

Now I'm startled by the phone in the house.

-Mother of God. I think it's important-, Can says with a sigh. -Do you mind if I answer it?

171

-Of course not.

We part ways. I close my eyes and breathe in and out. I hear Can in the distance. He's arguing with someone.

-Okay, I'm coming.

He walks over to me and picks up the remote control.

-It's Deren. She tells me to turn on the news.

He turns on the TV and I gasp as I recognize my face on the news. Can goes pale too.

-If true, this is unprecedented news with serious consequences for the projection of Turkish artists abroad-, says the anchorman. -For the moment, Can Divit has not issued any statement on the matter.

-Tell me what happened, Deren-, he demands. I've never seen him so enraged. Not even when he dragged me away from Mr. Fabri. -I see. From a year ago? That's impossible. Sanem and I did the photo shoot on the day of Fabri's party. Yes, don't answer to any reporters. I won't make any statements until I talk to my lawyer.

Hanging up, Can rubs his face. I forget my fears. Now it's Can who suffers and I don't understand why.

-What happened?

-An unknown website has appeared with your photos. Someone ti-pped off the press accusing me of plagiarism because, according to the website, your photos were published a year ago. This must be the work of a hacker. I don't understand how it happened.

-But no one could access the photos except us.

-Of course. There's a copy in my office, but it's locked in my safe and the only people who have had copies of the photos were you and Ilhan.

Can clenches his fists. His jaw tenses. I want to hug him, but I don't dare. There is one more person who saw the photos. I gave them to him, but Mr. Emre has not been able to betray his brother. I don't know anyone else who conspires against Can, though.

My palms sweat. What if Mr. Emre has been the spy all this time? I have sabotaged the company several times, albeit after the mole appeared and began to act. However, maybe I was the fool that Emre used to operate without suspicion.

-The only thing I can think of is that the spy stole the copy from my office and came up with this while we were publishing the campaign. Sanem, is your copy still safe?

-Yes. It's in my room.

-It could only have been the spy. That's the only explanation.

I went to Can's house to be honest with him. However, I lied to him again and what hurts me the most is that he never mistrusted me. I am stupid. They have deceived me as they have wanted.

-Emre and Deren are on their way. You should go, Sanem. I'm sorry I couldn't talk to you.

He accompanies me to the garden. There is no more playful teasing between us. He no longer seeks my eyes to dare me to talk to him. He doesn't hug me or assure me that everything will be all right. I want to stay by his side, but I don't deserve it. Maybe he should stay away from me. Right now talking to Emre is the only thing that will help me move forward.

At the bus stop I call him. I don't get an answer. I insist two, three times, enough times to make it clear that I won't stop until I talk to him.

-Sanem, what's wrong?

-Tell me you didn't leak the photos. It's not an order, but a plea.

-Of course not! Sanem, despite our differences, is my brother. It is one thing for him to sabotage his projects to prevent you from selling the company, but it is quite another to humiliate you on an international level. Sanem, this is going to be a very hard blow to his career.

-Only three of us knew about this project until I showed you the photos...

It's hard for me to say the word. The guilt eats away at my spirit.

-Sanem, I promise I will catch whoever is responsible.

-All right

I agree to believe him because it is the only thing I can do for the moment. I go back home. I don't turn on the TV because I will find my face on any channel. No neighbor in the neighborhood talks to me, except Ayhan, who is aware of how much this affects me. I use her shoulder as a refuge, but nothing lasts forever and my friend returns home. I remain alone, like Can. How will he feel now? Is this what they call love? Missing him as soon as you part from him. To think of him and carry his smile always in your heart. To feel his sorrow as your own. To leave when he asks you to and to stay if he wants you to. It is to over-understand his words. Is love a lot of questions, who am I, who is he? He held my hand and then told me to leave, is he the evil king or is he the dashing prince? His eyes burn with anger and he suffers like a wounded tiger. He won't let anyone near him... and I, I just want to hold him, to hold him in my arms, but I can't, at least not until I find out who has betrayed his trust.

In the office, our first job is to ignore the press. Dozens of journalists crowd the entrance, demanding that Can give his side of the story. Our boss has asked us to ignore them and has locked himself in his office.

At noon, Mr. Ilhan shows up here. He talks to Deren and Emre first. Then they all meet together in Can's office. I don't know what they are discussing. However, I know from their expressions that they have no clue as to the whereabouts of the person responsible. Before leaving, however, Mr. Ilhan approaches my desk.

-Sanem, I have spoken to Can-, he whispers confidentially. -We think the spy may have stolen the photos by stealing them from the safe or getting hold of some of the copies. Do you know if anything out of the ordinary has happened? With your copies or during the session with Can.

-No-, I say. I have a little trust left in Mr. Emre and that's why I don't tell on him. Or rather, I don't tell on us. -Is there no way to find out what happened?

-Not legally, no. However, we have also considered the possibility that this is the work of a hacker who broke into our system while we were setting up the campaign. With the website and a good hacker, we would trace it back to the culprit, but Can doesn't want to get into any more legal trouble.

Mr. Ilhan thinks he has failed to cheer me up. On the contrary, he has shown me the means by which I can help Can. Luckily, Ayhan knows a lot of people through her work as a personal coach.

As I leave the office, I call her on the phone.

-Ayhan, I need a favor.

-Sure, ask me anything you want.

-I need you to find a good hacker to track down the website where my photos appear.

-My God. Are you sure, Sanem? Hiring a hacker is no small feat. It's the underworld. We could get into trouble.

-I'll take responsibility. And if there's a meeting with the hacker, I'll ask an office mate to go with us.

Ayhan hesitates, but in the end my determination convinces her. My friend will move heaven and earth until she finds a hacker who will reveal the identity of the person who has destroyed Can's life. Time is against us. In the afternoon, I learned from Güliz that, until the matter is resolved and the accusations of plagiarism are dropped against Can, the International Photography Association has expelled him. It is a hard blow to his reputation and, although he pretends that nothing is happening, his rage is perceived in every gesture of pain and frustration that he unconsciously shows to others.

CHAPTER XXI

Ayhan has met my expectations and in two days she has found a reputable hacker in the underworld. My idea was to go with her to the computer scientist's base, but on the day we agreed to visit the hacker, Mr. Can disappeared.

Several Turkish institutions have withdrawn public support for him and many companies are considering dropping their sponsorship of the Divit studio. Now I can't abandon Can, so I ask Ceycey to accompany Ayhan to the hacker's neighborhood. My friend is not very happy to participate in such a mission, but when I introduced him to Ayhan, he pulled himself together and promised me that he would stay with her until the end.

While they follow the trail of the hacker who designed the website, I head for the cabin in the forest. If no one finds Can, it's probably because he has taken refuge there.

The journey is not easy because I lack a car and have had to resort to a cab. My efforts have been fruitless, though. There is no trace of Can in the hut. I don't know where else to turn because my boss hasn't confided any more details of his privacy, so I decide to return home. Luckily, for once fate decides to lend me a hand and Can's SUV crosses my path. I recognize it by the license plate and once again I give thanks for my photographic memory.

I ask the cab driver to drop me off and, without fear of getting lost, I go into the mountain. Can's car is parked next to a hiking trail, so I assume he's gone to stretch his legs.

I call out for Can and describe him to all the hikers I meet. No one has seen him and, although many insist that I don't go any further into the forest because it's easy to get lost, I don't follow the advice and go deeper and deeper into the thicket.

I feel like a heroine in a fairy tale looking for her beloved in the most remote place. Gradually it gets dark and I hear the owls singing, but I will not give up. Somewhere in this forest, Can has decided to hide to face his pain and I am going to accompany him in his sorrow. He was always with me in the moments when I found myself desolate at work. This is the time to show him that he can trust me.

In the end, just when I thought I was more likely to be eaten by a wolf than to find Can, my boss surprises me by appearing from behind.

-Sanem? What are you doing here?

It's worth the scare to be able to see him in front of me. If I get closer, he's within arm's reach. I want to hug him. However, now is not the time.

-Mr. Can. Deren and your brother are looking for you. Tomorrow you have to give a press conference.

-I already told Emre that I'm not going to talk to anyone. I'm innocent and I won't justify myself.

-But, Mr. Can, now people are preying on you like hyenas. The truth must be known.

Can smiles at me. Since the scandal began, he hasn't smiled tenderly at me.

-You're as precious as a shooting star, Sanem-, he flatters me, making me blush. -Come with me. It's late and it's dangerous to walk in the woods at night.

I accept and Can leads me to a small camp with a tent and campfire. I wonder how Ayhan and Ceycey are doing. If the hacker is as talented as his reputation claims, tomorrow Can could organize another press conference to prove his innocence with evidence.

-Are you hungry?-, he asks, offering me some roast beef.

After walking for hours in the forest, that piece of meat seems like a divine delicacy. While I eat, Can amuses himself by clinking two pebbles in his hand. They are the same ones he calmed himself down with when I drove the car at tortoise speed to Asmara.

-Are they special? The stones.

For a moment, Can looks out of place, but then he smiles and holds out his strange charms to me.

-They are a gift from an old woman I met on one of my trips. They represent the two faces of the moon: the white one is the visible one and the black one is the hidden one. They always guide me when I am confused.

All of Can's stories have a magical halo. I give him back the stones. On the one hand, I want to tell him about the task I gave Ayhan and Ceycey, but I dare not give him false hope. I still don't know if the hacker will manage to find the trail of whoever designed the fake website.

-Thank you for your concern for me, Sanem-, says Can, breaking the silence.

-It's no trouble-, I assure him. -You have always been very generous to me. You have encouraged me on so many occasions. It's the least I can do.

-Thank you-, he repeats.

The silence is pleasant. By the campfire there are no words. We have enough with the presence of the other. We contemplate the moon and the stars, the soft dance of the fire. I would love to stay with Can until dawn, though tiredness takes its toll on me. My eyelids grow heavier and heavier.

-Since I was planning to camp alone, the tent is too small-, Can tells me. Sleep there and rest. Tomorrow I'll wake you up to leave.

-Are you going to sleep out in the open?

-I'm used to it. This forest is very quiet. I've slept in worse places.

Even if you pretend you don't mind, I won't let you sleep alone on the ground.

-I can put the bag here and we can share the pillow.

-Sanem, don't...

-I insist.

Can behaves docilely for once and, between the two of us, we arrange the sleeping bag by the campfire. With Can by my side, the tiredness disappears. Turning my face, I feel his breath directly on my skin.

-Good night, Sanem.

-Good night, Mr. Can.

I didn't tell Mom I was sleeping outside. I'll get a good scolding, but I'll take my punishment. To experience this with Can is priceless.

In the morning I am awakened by the sound of Can taking down the tent. I stretch out. It's my first night outdoors and I've slept like a dormouse.

-Good morning, Sanem.

I'm glad to see that Can doesn't let himself get discouraged even though everything around him is falling apart. He still has sweetness reserved for me and I feel useful. I have not confessed my feelings to him, but I have done better. I have shown them.

Out of curiosity, I look at my cell phone. There is a message from Ayhan and another from Leyla. The one from my sister is unimportant because she assures me that she won't have my back anymore. I don't know if Ayhan has spoken to her, since I told my friend that I planned to look for Can for as long as it took.

Forgetting about my sister, I focus on my friend's message and as I read it my heart skips a beat.

"We have located the one who spoofed the website. Ceycey and I are going to see him in the morning. I'll pass on his address, but our hacker says this guy only takes assignments, so we're going to ask him who hired him."

I find it hard to hide my smile from Can, but I don't want to say anything to him until there's no certainty that we're going to catch the culprit.

-Excuse me, Mr. Can. I'm going to call my sister.

-Of course. I'm sorry for the inconvenience I've caused you.

In the car, driving back to the office, since we won't have time to stop by the house, I dial Leyla's number.

-Sanem, don't let this become a habit-, was her greeting. -Thank God I met Ayhan yesterday, otherwise I would have had a heart attack.

-I'm sorry, Leyla. It won't happen again.

-I'd like to believe you. Well, did you find your boss?

-Yes. We're on our way to the office right now because we have a press conference to give. I'll see you in the afternoon.

-Okay. I can't wait to strangle you.

-I love you too, Leyla.

Mr. Can has remained impassive during the conversation, but then he looks at me with the smirk I love so much.

-Family problems?

-Not much. My sister has had my back, although this is the second time she's done it in a short time.

-What was the first?

-The day of Mr. Fabri's party.

Can bursts out laughing. I almost cried with emotion. After having witnessed his sadness, this outburst of joy is a godsend.

-I'm afraid I'm not a good influence on you. I should behave better from now on.

-It's my fault. I should have warned her in advance and not in the morning of the next day.

-At least she takes care of you. Is she your big sister?

-Yes, she is.

-In my case it was Emre who pulled my chestnuts out of the fire even though he is the youngest-, he confesses, and at the mention of it, I consider telling Emre about my inquiries.

-He is a great man. By the way, Mr. Can, I would like to ask you to give me the day off if it is not too much trouble. I must take care of some business I neglected yesterday.

-Of course, Sanem. No problem.

Mr. Can drops me off near my neighborhood, as he has to get to the office early so as not to miss the press conference. I walk to the address Ayhan gave me in her message and in the meantime I call Mr. Emre.

-Good morning, Sanem. What's going on?

-We have found the hacker who set up the website-, I inform him. -We are on our way there right now to get the name of the person who hired him because we think he only did one assignment.

-My God, Sanem. I congratulate you. You are unbelievable.

I have never heard Mr. Emre so enthusiastic. He is a restrained gentleman and never shows his feelings too much. That's why his compliments please me so much.

-I'll pass on the address if you want to go-, I say.

-Of course. Does Can know anything?

-Not at the moment. I'd rather wait until I get the name of the culprit.

-Yes, that's best. When you get the address of whoever hired the hacker, text it to me. I'll forward it to Can at that time as well.

-I will, Mr. Emre.

I run down the street, jumping for joy. I just checked that Emre is not the one behind the website plot and I sigh with relief. I have not betrayed Can's trust. Instead, I'm going to thank him for everything he's done for me so far.

When I'm halfway there, I get a call from Ayhan. I tremble with excitement as I pick up.

-Sanem, we've already visited the other hacker.

-So soon?-, I'm surprised. I didn't realize Ayhan was so committed to the mission.

-Yes. Ceycey insisted on going first thing in the morning. This is a crazy job. Can you believe the hacker I contacted yesterday was only fifteen years old? Ceycey started making fun of him and I stopped him before he hacked into our bank accounts or worse.

-Seriously, Ayhan. You're the best friend in the world.

-I'm telling you-, she sighs. -Our hacker would be fifteen, but he lives in a rough neighborhood. Ceycey got scammed out of a hundred lira for asking for a simple address. Well, I'm going for a drink with Ceycey, who insists on inviting me for coffee. I'll text you the address of the person who hired the hacker. Do you need anything else?

-It's all done, Ayhan. I love you-, I confess with a beaming smile.

-Tell that to your albatross or Mr. Can-, she chides me, but after this I plan to tell him the truth. I will tell him that I love him. So as not to make him dizzy with Mr. Emre's shenanigans, I will tell him that I have broken up with Osman and then there will be nothing to come between us.

After saying goodbye to Ayhan, I call Mr. Emre again.

-Have you got any news yet, Sanem?

-Yes. He passed her the address of the person who hired the hacker.

-Wonderful, Sanem. You are just wonderful. I warn Can and head there right away. Be careful.

-I will, Mr. Emre.

After mentioning it, I realize that I will not succeed in reducing the culprit of this disgusting operation, so I wait at the address Ayhan gave me until Emre appears. As usual, he shows up in his brand new sports car. Today, however, he looks different. I've never seen him so active.

-Have you contacted the suspect?

-No-, I confess. Since I don't know who he is, I decided to wait for him. However, I have been watching and no one has entered or left the house.

-Perfect-, Emre says to me.

He leads the way. The address points to a small house, a townhouse. It's a neighborhood similar to mine, perhaps a bit more humble. Whoever lived there was not a big businessman, so it could be someone dangerous. Despite that, Emre knocks decisively on the door.

We wait expectantly. To my surprise, a small man in pajamas opens the door. He looks at us with surprise and a slight sense of fear. I get brave and push open the door, as Emre is petrified.

-Are you responsible for the set-up against Can Divit?-, I ask, as if to acknowledge his guilt. Sometimes I am too naive, but to my surprise, the man flees in terror, confirming our suspicions.

Recovering, Emre roughly pushes me away and runs towards the scoundrel. He tries to hide in his room, but Can's brother prevents him by ramming the door. The beast almost rips it off its hinges.

-What have you done?-, He reproaches the stranger with an aggressiveness that scares even me.

-I, I'm not to blame. Really...

Emre pushes him against the bed in his room. If he hadn't tried to destroy Can's life, I would feel sorry for the bastard.

-Sanem-, Emre then says, looking me in the eye. There is so much anger in his eyes that I feel fear and, for some strange reason, guilt as well.

-What's wrong?

Emre swallows saliva. He shies away from my gaze. He is embarrassed. Please don't let him say anything.

-I hired this man to manage the web setup.

I faint. I have to hold on to something to keep from falling.

-In theory, I paid him to travel abroad, but the idiot didn't do it.

-You can't be behind all this. I believed you...

My body trembles, my eyes sting. However, anger soon replaces weakness.

-You have deceived me all this time!-, I yell. -When I met Can, I was surprised that he wasn't like you told me, but I believed you and worked for you!

-Sanem, listen.

-He's your brother! How could you do that?!

I want to run away from here. To run to Can and cry on his chest. But Emre cuts me off.

-Sanem, you don't understand.

-Of course I don't! I've never met anyone so low!

Emre trembles too. If I don't slam him against the wall, it's because I'm afraid of him. He's not who I thought he was. I don't know how he will react if I try to get rid of him. Besides, embarrassment weakens my steps. I get dizzy.

-What are you going to do?

-Tell Mr. Can the truth. He deserves to know.

-Oh, does he?-, He steps forward to face me. -So tell him everything. Tell him how you sabotaged all his projects and betrayed his trust.

-You're despicable-, I say, though that doesn't mean I'm not, too.

-That's the way of the world, Sanem.

-I don't care. Mr. Can deserves to know the truth. I'm going to tell him everything.

I'm going to do it. I'll be brave for once in my life. I'll prove that my love is sincere.

-Sanem, what's wrong? What do you have to tell me?

My heart stops. Mr. Emre pales as if Can is his executioner. We both turn to him and at that moment we realize that the man who hired the hacker is also in the room. We were so immersed in our discussion that neither of us noticed what was going on around us.

-We've found the man responsible for setting up the website-, says Emre before I can recover.

Furious, Can turns to the one who in reality is just a mere puppet who has participated in this farce.

-What's your problem with me?

If Emre used to inspire fear, Can now instills dread in anyone in his presence. I lower my head. If he looks at me, he'll find out that I've been a part of this too and he'll hate me forever.

I am so mentally exhausted that I don't react in time when the stranger starts to run and pushes me away. I hit my head against a pillar and fall almost faint.

Can screams my name. I hear Mr. Emre curse. My knight lifts me in his arms and carries me to the couch. How will I tell you that I am not worthy of you?

-Sanem, don't exert yourself. It's over-, he whispers to me with a tenderness that only makes me want to cry.

He takes care of me. He reaches for a handkerchief, wraps ice in it and presses it to the bruise on my head. I feel like vomiting. I hate this feeling.

After a few minutes, Emre returns with his puppet and throws it on the floor. Can stops paying attention to me and runs over to the man and slams him against the wall.

-If anything happens to the girl, I'll kill you. Do you hear me?!

-Calm down, Can. I've called the police-, Emre intervenes.

-I don't care-, he threatens, raising his fist. His victim shrinks back. He is not the one who should be on the receiving end of Can's wrath. Emre and I are the ones who deserve the punishment.

-Can, when we talk to the police, you will regain your prestige and your name will be cleared. Don't lose that for revenge. You are worth more than that-, says the hypocrite. -Take care of Sanem, she needs you.

I don't hate Mr. Emre as much as I despise myself. Can has never been a wicked king, but the fairest knight I have ever known and if rage now dominates him it is because he cares for me and because he wishes to release all the stress he has accumulated these days for us.

Can watches over me. Emre watches over his prey and me. It is not necessary for now. I am a coward and do not wish to lose Can's caresses. On the one hand, they keep me from losing my mind. On the other, they remind me how despicable I am.

When the police arrive and take the statement of the one who is going to pay for Emre's wickedness, he stands next to me.

-What are you going to say, Sanem?

I cry.

-You disgust me. So, you have convinced this man to pay for you?

-I'll see to it that he doesn't suffer a very severe punishment.

187

I tremble with rage. There is no justice in this world.

-My brother hates lies with all his being-, Emre explains to me. -That's what separated him from our mother before she died, and he has despised liars ever since. If you tell him the truth, neither of us can make peace with him.

He's so damn clever. He has caught me in his web. He knows my great weakness and he knows that, like him, I am a miserable coward.

-I'm going to tender my resignation and stay as far away from you as I can.

-It is not necessary, Sanem. If you don't say anything, I'll take care of everything. You don't have to lose your job.

Now you're playing at being sympathetic?

-What happens to me is my problem alone.

After taking a statement and asking about how the investigation would progress, Can comes back to us. He sits down next to me and whispers in my ear with the sweetness that always melts my heart.

-Don't worry, Sanem. Everything will be all right thanks to you. You are my hero.

I never imagined I would feel so much pain hearing those words spoken by Can.

CHAPTER XXII

In the newspapers there is no talk about anything other than the plot against Can Divit. The official version is that a former employee of his company decided to take revenge on him, but I know the truth. I am a faker. I have appeared in the media as the person who uncovered the frame-up and my fame is growing, partly also because of the campaign organized by Mr. Ilhan and Can.

Can is looking for me. He wants to hug me. He smiles at me. I run away from him. I accept the assignments Deren offers me, even the most humiliating ones, as long as I am not available. I can't go on like this, so three days after discovering I'm miserable, I meet with Mr. Emre.

-I'm resigning. I can't stand being here anymore. I won't keep pretending to others-, I tell him.

Emre doesn't answer me. He just takes out a check from his desk and signs a checkbook.

-Can told me you dream of becoming a writer. Take that money and make the most of it. Live your dream.

I take the check and tear it up in front of Emre.

-You are not going to buy my silence. I'm going to pay you back one by one the forty thousand lira you lent me.

-Sanem, please. Be reasonable.

-I am being reasonable for once in my life.

I take the ring out of my bag and put it on the table.

-Here you go. Will you at least be honest and tell me why I fooled everyone?

Emre picks up the ring, who was it originally for and why didn't he ever miss it? I can't quite make out his expression. He looks remorseful, but that's just one of his many masks.

-My brother was always my father's favorite. He entrusted him with running the studio even though he's spent his life traveling. That ended up driving a wedge between us and I ended up losing my mind.

-Can loves you.

-And I love him. Deep down, I didn't lie to you. He's my brother and I respect him. I never imagined it would end like this.

He plays with me. He manipulates me. He wants me to feel sorry for him and he's not going to get it. I come out of his office.

-Sanem!-, Can calls out to me. I have not had time to present myself to Deren to announce my resignation.

The perfect gentleman approaches me. He ignores that the woman he considers his heroine is a vile traitor.

-What's the matter, Sanem? You look very sad. Where is your ring?

-I broke up with Osman-, I say. I'm incorrigible. -Now I want to focus on helping my family with the butchery, so I'm resigning.

-With the butcher shop? I don't understand you, Sanem. You have a dream. You can do great things for it in this company. I promised you that you would write the script for our next film and now more than ever I intend to keep my promise. Please stay.

I cry. Can doesn't deserve to worry about someone like me.

-I have made my decision, Mr. Can. Thank you so much for everything you have done for me.

I break away from him with determination. I talk to Deren and notify her of my resignation. For once, she does not look at me with his expression of rejection and accepts my wish. She seems to want to tell me something. Nevertheless, we say goodbye with a simple goodbye.

-Deren, don't accept Sanem's resignation-, says Can in a tone of voice loud enough to be heard by several colleagues around me, including Ceycey and Güliz.

My friend runs to me.

-Resign? Sanem, you're going to start working as a designer. We already have enough material. Please don't be silly, little girl. Is it because of something I said? I won't mess with your taste in tea again.

Why do I only get love from others when I deserve contempt?

-It's not you, Ceycey. You're the best partner anyone could have. You're never going to get fired.

I run out of there before Güliz bombards me with questions about my decision. Can keeps calling me. I ignore him. I'm not going to look back. This world is not for me.

At home, my mother is surprised that I have returned so soon. She greets me and for a second glimpses my tears. She runs to my room, opens the door and hugs me.

-What's wrong with you, my child?

-I'm worthless, Mom. I'm completely useless-, I confess to her in tears.

-No, Sanem. You're not like that. You have a big heart and we all know it. There's no one in the neighborhood who speaks ill of you and I always brag about you to Aysun. Do you think that with the great daughter I have, I'm going to let her marry Misifu? Girl, you're worth a lot. You have a dream, a job where you do amazing things, and I know you will be the best writer in Istanbul.

No, please don't. I don't deserve this. I cry on my mother's shoulder and drown my sobs in her. We spend most of the morning like this and she only separates when Dad can replace her. I've confessed to them that I've resigned because I don't deserve this job and they don't know what to do. In the end, Mom calls Ayhan so I can unburden myself to her.

-Sanem, what's wrong? Come on, don't cry. Tell me everything.

My parents are downstairs. They will grant me privacy while I talk to Ayhan. So, I tell my friend how stupid I have been, how I have deceived Mr. Can and how I have received only his appreciation.

-Sanem, you love him and you are a good person. That's why it hurts you to have hurt him indirectly, but you have saved him and I bet my hand that his scoundrel of a brother won't dare to play with him again for a long time. Sanem, you are too good. Don't cry.

I refuse to believe her. I'm not worthy of anything. I take my notebook and throw it in the trash. I ignore Ceycey when she comes to ask me to return to the company. My friend tells me that everyone is expecting me back and that they miss me. Mr. Can has even given him hours off to come and talk to me.

-Sanem, I think deep down he feels guilty about something. He cares a lot about you.

Hearing that gives me the coup de grace. Can's kindness is overwhelming. There is no man like him. He looks like he just stepped out of a love story.

In the evenings I walk around the harbor, imagining what would have happened if Mr. Emre hadn't used me. Maybe now I would be talking to Can on a one-on-one basis. I could have told him that I love him and, perhaps, in the most beautiful dream in the world, he would have replied that he loves me too.

Once, under the full moon, I meet Can at the harbor. It is him. There is no doubt about it. He is the prince of stories and, as in fairy tales, the man I love has returned. He has missed me. He's a couple of steps away from me, but this story will not have a happy fairy tale ending. I am the evil character in this tale, I lied to a man who hates liars more than anything in the world, so I turn away. I walk away from him, without revealing the truth. Even if he hates them, it's better that he lives in lies. Let him think Osman has broken my heart and I can't go back to work.

It's better for everyone.

But what if love doesn't die? The days go by and this pain doesn't go away. Misifu takes the opportunity to try to woo me, Osman comes to visit me, listens to me cry and then hugs me. Dad always tries to cheer me up with jokes when I work with him in the butcher shop. Leyla encourages me to get back to work and keep writing. One day, she takes my notebook out of the wastebasket and puts it on the desk.

-If it goes back in the garbage can, I will always leave it there.

I'm going to give her three days to forget about it and then I'll throw it into the dock on one of my walks. Unfortunately, on the second day there is a visit that completely upsets me. Can Divit has come in person to give me a gift.

My parents receive him as usual. They invite him to dinner, but he assures me that he does not wish to disturb. He says he's just coming to leave me a gift. I hear his voice from my bedroom door.

-It's a farewell gift. I'm leaving in a few days-, he announces, and my chest heaves.

I can't imagine a world where I can't pass Can on the street because of a trick of fate.

-Sanem-, he greets me after climbing the stairs.

-What do you want, Can?

He holds out a gift to me. The shape is dear and familiar to me. The wrapping paper smells of his cologne.

-I don't know why, but I'm sorry if I hurt you. You've been avoiding me for days and now you've chosen to quit your job. Please don't give up your dreams. For a talent like yours to remain unpolished is a disgrace to the world.

I open the package. It is a beautiful notebook with a leather cover. Inside is an albatross pen for writing. I swallow saliva. It's hard to breathe.

-Even if I can't read your novel, I ask you to write it there. It would make me very happy.

-I can't write, Can.

-Of course you can. There's great creativity in everything you do. Do you think I haven't noticed? Every day I've worked with you, you've amazed me like no one else has ever done before. If you can't make up a story today, write about yourself. Use your memories. Change them as you wish to live your dream reality, but please don't waste your talent.

Tears run down my cheeks. Your words have been like a divine gift of inspiration. Pain cries out to me to write Mr. Can my love in fifty thousand different ways so as not to lose him. However, we say goodbye and he walks away.

I lock myself in my room. My mother has not come up to see me after the visit, though shortly afterward Ayhan knocks on my door and asks permission to enter. I grant it and she jumps on me.

-Seriously, the neighborhood is in an uproar at the sight of Can Divit. Misifu almost had a fit of jealousy right there. What did he want?

-To give me a parting gift.

-A parting gift? Speak now, young lady, or I'll beat the words out of you.

I hold out the notebook to her and tell her Can's words one by one.

-Sanem! Do you realize what a great man you've let go? If I already felt hot just looking at him, listening to what he says to you I dream of meeting one just like him.

-But that's all they are. Dreams. He's perfect, but he's not for me.

-Let's see, Sanem. I'm going to give you a free personal growth class because you're my friend. Nobody is perfect. We're the ones who have to improve day by day. Do you think Can Divit is flawless? I'm sure he has them. If not, he would be happily married to a dream woman right now, but sometimes when we meet someone we truly love, that person brings out the best in us and you have caused a Can that borders on perfection.

-Ayhan, I...

-Nothing. Right now, you're going to talk to him before he goes off to the ass end of the world so you don't have to think about his pain anymore. Did you hear what he said? He loves you. He loves you madly and he thinks he's hurt you and he can't take it. Are you going to let him think that? Because you wouldn't deserve it if you were capable of such cruelty.

I smile. Ayhan tickles me.

-You go out and I entertain your mother. It's late, but Osman can drive you to Can's house.

-Ayhan. I'm...

-You're like my sister. We grew up together. We know each other inside out.

I hug her. If I wrote a thousand different books, I would always put a friend like Ayhan in them. She always listens to me and knows how to encourage me to achieve my destiny. I say goodbye to her, and thank her from the bottom of my heart for taking off my blindfold, for allowing me to be a liar who deserves to love Mr. Can.

I run. I leave the house, crying again. My parents want to stop me because it's ten o'clock at night. However, Leyla steps in between them.

-Don't come back too late!

I run. My heart is going to explode. Feelings are overflowing. I have lied to Can. I'll probably keep doing it, but right now I'm at a crossroads with two stories. In one, I go to Can and confess my feelings. In the other, I pretend normalcy, go back to work, even Can can stay in the office because his old girlfriend, Polen, is back and encourages him not to leave. In that story, we can chase each other, play cat and mouse, make each other jealous. Me, looking for my albatross and pretending to find him in other men; him, staying with Polen and making me believe that his love story with her is perfect and is what he desires.

Mistrust is stupidity. I will make a thousand mistakes from now on. We will argue, but Can is not a dream character, he is someone real and I will not lose him. It's the truth, and the truth always disappoints you, but dreams are not real. In them everything is perfect, love is eternal and there is always happiness. When you are with the man you love you feel like you are living in a dream, but now you must put your dreams aside and believe in yourself. Be a new Sanem, a brave Sanem, master of her destiny.

Can is not perfect. Neither am I, but I write this story and I choose the best possible ending.

Osman offers me a ride to Can's house. He encourages me on the trip with his presence. We say nothing. I know we inspire each other. There is no one better to accompany me. Hopefully he will pluck up the courage and, when he returns and talks to Leyla to explain everything, he will confess his love to her as I am going to do now with Can.

I cross the garden. I approach the front door and knock. I gasp. My heart is about to burst and the door opens. And behind it is not his girl-friend Polen or anyone else who could come between us. There is only Can, who looks at me in astonishment.

-Sanem, what are you doing here?

I snort. I look at him and face him. Please look me in the eye this time. Let's both dare. And Can reads the truth in my eyes. This is not a lie and, grabbing my arms, he kisses me. I recognize this feeling of love, these arms muscles around me. We are no longer at a gala party. We have met again, but not in an exceptional circumstance, but in an ordinary night like any other. A real night like our love.

As we part. I can't believe what has just happened. He smiles at me and caresses my cheek.

-Albatross?

He nods and kisses me again to confirm.

-How? Since when?

-Since always, dear Sanem.

-But the albatross can't be Mr. Can. Or can it?

His laughter washes away all my fear and pain. The past no longer matters, only the present.

-I am not Mr. Can. I am Can. Just Can.

He hugs me. My hands tremble. He picks them up gently and kisses them.

-Don't go, Can. I don't want to part from you.

He holds me tighter in his arms.

-I won't leave if you don't want me to, Sanem.

I still can't believe this is the reality. Can is my beloved albatross. He gave me a pen and his last name means "Inkwell". How poetic...

I close my eyes, not thinking about what the future holds. Now I am a majestic bird, radiant with light, the phoenix that rises from its ashes and flies towards tomorrow in the company of my albatross.

This is reality, my story. It is not a dream, so I am glad because my love will continue without fear that it will disappear if I wake up.

TABLE OF CONTENT